Alighieri Dante

Dante's Divina Commedia

Translated Into English

Alighieri Dante

Dante's Divina Commedia
Translated Into English

ISBN/EAN: 9783337145545

Printed in Europe, USA, Canada, Australia, Japan

Cover: Foto ©Andreas Hilbeck / pixelio.de

More available books at **www.hansebooks.com**

DANTE'S
DIVINA COMMEDIA.

TRANSLATED INTO ENGLISH,

IN THE METRE AND TRIPLE RHYME
OF THE ORIGINAL.

WITH NOTES

BY

MRS. RAMSAY.

Purgatorio.

LONDON:
TINSLEY BROTHERS, 18, CATHERINE ST., STRAND.
1862

LONDON
BRADBURY AND EVANS, PRINTERS, WHITEFRIARS

THE
DIVINE COMEDY OF DANTE.

PURGATORIO.

CANTO I.

Argument

Dante, having come forth from the dark cavern, gazes with wonder and delight at the starry sky, and sees for the first time the constellation of the Southern Cross.—Discourse with Cato of Utica, guardian of Purgatory.

Now let my fancy's ship unfurl her sail,

Her course o'er smoother waters to begin,

And leave behind her all the sea of wail ;

And of that second kingdom will I sing,

Where pain each mortal spirit purifies

Ere it can upward soar on heavenward wing.

Here let my Lay from Death once more arise,

O Muses, since to you do I belong,

And here Calliope in tuneful guise

   Appear, and bring with her, to aid my song,

The selfsame melody which erst they knew

Who mourn, as chattering jays, their hopeless wrong

   The oriental sapphire's lovely hue

That colour'd the pure air, serenely bright,

O'erspreading all the sky with deepest blue,

   Again unto mine eyes brought back delight ;

Soon as the deathly air I rose above,

The air that grieved my heart and dimm'd my sight.

   The beauteous planet, counsellor of love,

Arose and shed o'er all the east her smile,

Hiding the Fish that in her escort move

   To the right hand I turn'd, and gazed awhile

At the far pole, and saw four stars, unseen

By man since sin our parents did beguile.

   Their radiance gladden'd all the sky, I ween :

O region of the Northland, cold and gray,

Since parted from their brightness thou hast been !

   I turn'd from gazing at the holy ray ;

A little towards the north my glance was thrown,

There where the Wain but now had pass'd away.

I saw anear me an old man alone ;
To whom so much of reverence seem'd due,
As to a father by his own is shown.

His beard was long, and miz'd with hoary hue,
And like unto the flowing locks he wore,
That, double-falling, both his shoulders strew.

The holy radiance of the starry Four
Shed on his forehead such a dazzling beam,
It seem'd as though the sun's own light he wore.

"And who are ye that, 'gainst Hell's sluggish stream,
From the eternal prisonhouse have fled ?"
He spake, and shook his hair of silvery gleam ;

"Who is your guide ? and who the light that led
Forth from the night of everlasting gloom,
That darkens aye the valley of the dead ?

Or broken are the laws of final doom ?'
And is there now new counsel in the sky,
That even the damn'd to my abode should come ?"

My Master then made signs with hand and eye,
Exhorting me to make obeisance low,
And to the ancient sage bend rev'rently ;

Then answer'd : " Not at mine own will I go ,

A Blessèd One descended from above,
To send me as a guide through realms of woe.

But since of our condition thou wouldst prove
The truth still more, I may not say thee nay,
Nor may my will against thy wishes move.

This man hath never seen the closing day
Of life ; but in his madness drew so nigh,
That little time remain'd to turn away.

As I have said, a Lady from on high
Commanded me to aid him , and no place
Of flight remain'd, save that we have pass'd by.

And I have show'd him all the wicked race,
And now would lead him through the spirit throng,
Who 'neath thy guardianship their sins efface.

To tell thee all our journey were too long ;
Know, from above hath heavenly virtue flow'd,
That for this enterprise doth make me strong.

Now deign to welcome him to thy abode ;
He goes to seek for liberty —so dear
As he who gives his life for it hath show'd :

And thou must know it well, who hadst no fear
Of death in Utica ;—where thou hast shed

The vesture that in glory shall appear

   At the last day. Heaven's edicts are not made

In vain for us. This man hath mortal life ;

And I am of that region of the dead,

   Where she, who was on earth thy loving wife,

Still loves thee in the land of shadowy woe :

For her sake, then, befriend us in our strife.

   Let me throughout thy sevenfold kingdom go ;

To her I will take back a good report,

If thou wouldst be remember'd there below."

   " Marcia to me such gladness did impart

On earth," he said, " that, whatsoe'er she would,

I did ; so dear was she unto my heart.

   Now that she dwells beyond the evil flood,

She cannot move me more ; by that decree

Made when my soul forth issued with my blood.

   If sent by heavenly messenger ye be,

As thou hast said, no need of flattering speech ;

Enough that in such name thou askest me.

   Go then, descend unto the salt sea beach,

And gird this wand'rer with the reeds that rise

Beside the wave ; and wash the stains that reach

O'er all his visage : lest that, with his eyes
Dimm'd by'some cloud, he should appear before
The angel minstrant of Paradise.

For all around this little island shore,
Down where the waters beat upon the strand,
There springs of reeds and rushes ample store.

No other plant may blossom 'mid the sand ;
No stem resist the dashing of the main :
None that unto the billows doth not bend.

By this same path return ye not again ;
The sun, that now is rising, be your guide
More easily the summit to attain."

He vanish'd : silent I drew near the side
Of him who led me through the lake of woe.
Thus to my mute enquiry he replied :

" My son, do thou behind my footsteps go ;
Let us turn back, for this way it must be,
The plain descends unto the waves below."

The dawn was conquering the mists that flee
Before it, as the early shadows wane ,
Afar I knew the trembling of the sea.

We pass'd along the solitary plain,

As one who turns again to the lost way,
And, till he finds it, seems to walk in vain.   120

   When we were come to where the dewdrops lay,
Despite the sun (because on the long reeds
But little had the freshness pass'd away),

   Then both his hands upon the scatter'd weeds
Softly my Master laid among the dew :   125
And I, who knew his meaning and my needs,

   Bent unto him my cheeks of tearful hue ;
While the dark stains he wash'd away, that bore
The impress of the hell I had pass'd through.

   Now we were come unto the desert shore   130
Of that great sea, upon whose waters wide
He who hath sail'd returns again no more.

   There was I clothèd by my gentle guide :
And then, in sooth, a wondrous thing was seen ;
Swift as he pluck'd it, by the flowing tide,   135

   Again the lowly plant sprang up, in freshest green

CANTO II.

—·—

Argument

Dante perceives a bark guided by a white winged angel, and
bearing the souls to Purgatory.—Among them he discovers
his friend Casella, who by his melodious song causes the
Shades to forget their destination.—Anger of Cato.

The sun now low on the horizon lay,

On the horizon of the Holy Land,

Shedding on Sion's mount the close of day;

And Night, who aye opposed to him doth stand,

Came slowly forth from out the Ganges stream,

Bearing the balances, that from her hand

At midnight fall : and thus the rosy gleam,

Tinging the cheeks of the fair Nymph of Day,

All changed to orange hue to us did seem.

And still beside the shore did we delay,

As those who musing would their path discern,

Go with their heart and with their footsteps stay.

And lo! as, near the dawning of the morn,
Through the thick vapour Mars, with redder light,
Shines in the west, above the watery bourne,

I saw (and would 'twere now within my sight,)
A star come swiftly tow'rds us o'er the sea;
Faster it sped than any arrow's flight.

One moment at my guide I glanced, that he
Might with his wisdom aid my weaker thought;
More large and bright the vision seem'd to be.

Now on each side appear'd I know not what
Of white; and as the vessel nearer drew,
Beneath, meseem'd, another form it brought.

My guide was silent, till at last he knew
The bark that sped on its uncarthly road,
Borne by those wings of white and glistening hue.

He cried: " Now lowly kneel upon the sod;
Behold a heavenly angel; fold thy hands;
For thou shalt see the messenger of God.

Lo! for his wondrous voyage he demands
Nor oar, nor sail, nor any means of flight,
Save his own wings, between each distant strands.

See how he spreads them tow'rds the fount of light,

Those pinions which unchanged do ever wear,
Unlike to human locks, their freshness bright.

  Now, as the bird of heaven to us drew near,
The dazzling radiance lighten'd more and more,
Till human eye the splendour might not bear,

  But sank to earth.   Softly he touch'd the shore,
With his light shallop gliding o'er the flood,
That gently still its charmed burden bore ;

  And at the helm the angel pilot stood,
With blessedness inscribed upon his brow.
More than a hundred souls there were who would

  Here wash away their mortal stains : and now
" *In exitu* " they sang , as with one voice
Did all the psalm in sweetest music flow.

  And then he made the sign of Holy Cross ;
Wherefore they gladly sprang upon the strand :
And, as he came, so swiftly did he pass.

  With shy and timid aspect did the band,
Left on a stranger shore, look round each way,
As one who would some new thing understand.

  The sun was shooting down the burning day,
The fiery darts with which his skilful bow

From half the sky had chased the Goat away:

  Turning towards us with uplifted brow

The wand'rers newly landed from the sea

Of us the way to climb the mount would know.

  And Virgil answered : " It well may be,

Ye think we have experience of this land ;

But we are also pilgrims even as ye.

  A little while before you, we did wend

Hither our way along a path so rude

That now this seemeth easy to ascend."

  The souls, who by my breathing understood

That yet I had not seen the mists of death,

All wonderstruck remain'd, and pale and mute :

  And as to him who wears an olive wreath,

To hear glad tidings all the people flow,

Each trampling each, so fast he hasteneth :

  Now unto me those blessed souls even so.

Drew near ; and in their eagerness forgot

That they to wash away their stains must go.

  And one advanced as to embrace me, fraught

With such deep tenderness in all his mien,

It moved my heart to the like gentle thought.

O Shades, in all but in the aspect vain !
Three times around his form my arms I threw ;
Thrice they return'd to my own breast again.

I think my cheek with wonder changed its hue ,
Wherefore the shadow smiled, and drew away ;
And I, who follow'd him, pass'd onward too.

Gently he said to me that I should stay ;
And then I knew him, and I begg'd that he
To speak with me a little would delay.

He said : " As was in life my love to thee,
It is the same in death ; therefore I stop :
But tell me wherefore may thy coming be ? "

I said : " My own Casella, for the hope
Here to return again ; but why so long
Hast thou delay'd to reach thy journey's scope ? "

And he to me : " No one hath done me wrong,
If he, that (whom and whom he will) doth bear
Unto this blessèd isle the spirit throng,

Hath still denied the voyage unto my prayer.
His will is ever just.—Three months have fled,
Since all who would may freely enter here ;

And I, who in that region of the dead

Was left, where Tiber to the sea doth flow,
At last benignly to this shore was led.

   Again toward that stream his pinions go,
For waiting ever on its strand are found
Those who descend not to the shades below."

   " If the decrees by which thou here art bound,"
I said, " have left remembrance of the strain
That used to calm my spirit with sweet sound,

   Then with its melody console again
My heart, which, passing through such scenes of ill,
In coming here hath suffer'd many a pain."

   " Love that within my soul discourseth still,"
Thus he began ; so musical the lay
Its sweetness yet my memory doth fill.

   And ever listening, both we and they
Who with the minstrel were, seem'd so content
As care for aught besides had pass'd away.

   And still we stood, all silent and intent
Upon his notes : when lo ! the sage, who cries :
" Wherefore do ye delay the steep ascent,

   O indolent and slothful ?   Now arise ;
Fly to the mount to wash away the slime

Which hides the Eternal Spirit from your eyes."

Even as the doves in pleasant harvest time,
To feed upon the golden grain unite,
Silent, without their wonted murmuring rhyme ;

If aught appear that causes them affright,
Sudden they let their food untasted stand,
Because on them a greater care doth light:

Thus did I see the new-come pilgrim-band
(As one who goes, unheeding of the way)
Leaving the music, fly towards the strand :

Nor were we less intent on hasty flight than they.

CANTO IIL

Argument

Dante and Virgil endeavour to find the upward path — Meeting
with Manfred, King of Sicily

ALTHOUGH the suddenness with which we fled
Had scatter'd all the wanderers, who now
Turn'd to the mount again where reason led,

  Still to my faithful guide I clung, for how,
Without his aid, could I have held my course?
Who would have dragg'd me up the mountain's brow?

  He seem'd in his own thoughts to feel remorse:
O conscience quick and pure, that even the least,
The slightest fault dost bitterly rehearse!

  Now when his steps had ceased from the haste,
Befitting ill the form of Majesty,
My mind, that all within itself was placed,

Again look'd forth, as eager to espy
The road by which we took our rugged way,
From out the waves ascending to the sky.

The sun, whose crimson flame behind us lay,
No light before me on the path had thrown;
Because upon my form it found a stay:

I turn'd in dread to find myself alone;
For I perceived no shadow by my side,
And deem'd, perchance, my comforter was gone.

But he, all turn'd towards me, thus replied:
" Why are thy thoughts within thee thus at war?
Believ'st me not still with thee as thy guide?

In Naples now beneath the vesper star,
My body lies, that threw on earth a shade;
Erst was it brought from Brindisi afar

If here no shadow by my form is made,
Thou shouldst not marvel more than at the skies,
Because on them the sunbeams are not stay'd.

To bodies of like nature, the Allwise
Hath given to suffer torments, heat and cold ·
How this may be is hidden from our eyes.

Your mortal intellect is all too bold,

And finite would the Infinite discern,

That in Three Persons doth one substance hold.

But ye the cause from the effect must learn,

If to the whole your human glance might soar,

It needed not that Mary's Son be born

Nor had ye seen, on the eternal shore,

Some, whose vain longing for the good they seek

Is given to them as grief for evermore.

Of Aristotle and Plato do I speak,

And many others." Then his head he bent,

In sorrow; nor again did silence break.

Meanwhile unto the mountain foot we went,

And there so steep the precipice around,

In vain to climb it would our strength be spent.

Between Turbia and Lerici's bound,

Each rocky path, most difficult and high,

Compared with this, a gentle slope were found.

"Now who can tell us where the way may lie,'

My Master said, as he his footsteps stay'd,

"That he may climb who hath no wings to fly?"

And downward, as in thought, he bent his head,

Deep musing on the dangers of the place,

While to the rocky height my glances stray'd.

At the left hand I saw appear a race
Of spirits, who towards us did advance ;
But seemed not to move, so slow their pace.

I to my Master said : " Uplift thy glance ;
Lo ! they who will give counsel now appear,
If thine own thoughts have need of aid perchance."

Then he look'd up, and with an aspect clear,
Replied " Come tow'rds them, for they linger long ;
And thou, my gentle son, be of good cheer."

And still so distant from us was their throng,
After a thousand paces we had trod,
As might a stone be cast by marksman strong,

When to the rocky wall that edged the road
They all drew near ; and motionless remain'd,
As one who doubts what some new thing may bode.

" O spirits who this blessed isle have gain'd,"
Virgil began, " I pray you, by that peace
I well believe ye all shall have attain'd

At last, now tell us where these ramparts cease,
So that we may ascend the rugged steep ;
For loss of time the wise doth most displease."

As from the pen come forth the timid sheep,
Some two or three ; the rest, with aspect shy,
Bent to the earth their eyes and noses keep ;

All that the foremost does, the others try,
And when he stops, still close behind they stand,
Simple and quiet, nor know the reason why :

Thus did I see the leader of that band
Approach to meet us on our onward way,
With modest air.   And as on my right hand,

Even to the rock the dusky shadow lay,
As though my form had quench'd the solar flame,
Amazed at that strange sight their steps they stay.

Those who were nearest us, no farther came ;
And all the rest who in their footsteps went,
Although they know not wherefore, did the same.

" He upon whom ye now are so intent
Is in the body death shall yet receive ;
Therefore the sunny light on earth is spent.

Be not so struck with wonder ; but believe,
Not without strength that cometh from on high
This rampart's outer circle would he cleave :"

The Master spake.   And thus was the reply :

" Return with us again, by the same part
Ye come from ;" and they sign'd with hand and eye.

Then one of them begun : " Whoe'er thou art,
Still ever journeying onward, turn thee now ;
Hast thou not seen me when on earth thou wert ?"

I turn'd and look'd on him with stedfast brow ;
Fair was his aspect and of gentle mien ;
But on his forehead was a deadly blow.

I humbly answer'd, never had I seen
His form till now ; and then he show'd the trace
Where on his breast a mortal wound had been.

" Know, I am Manfred, of imperial race,"
He smiling said , " and when thou dost resume
Thine earthly life within its wonted place,

Unto my daughter go, to her of whom
Are sprung the kings of Sicily and Spain :
Tell her the truth of me and of my doom.

After my lifeblood had gush'd forth like rain,
From two deep wounds, my soul I weeping gave
To him who gladly cleanseth every stain.

In life my sins did God's great judgments brave ;
But yet his arms of tender love embrace

All who return to him before the grave.

And if Cosenza's pastor, sent in chase

Of me by Clement, had but rightly known   125

How of the mind of God to read this face,

My body still were where it first was thrown,

Above the bridge anear to Benevent,

Well guarded by the heavy pile of stone.

Now it is beaten by the rain, and rent   130

By storm, afar where Verde's wave is seen,

Where from the realm 'twas borne with torches spent

For curse of theirs one is not lost, I ween,

They cannot turn away the love of God,

While hope still bears its blossoms, fresh and green.   135

Who dies in the contempt that he hath show'd

For Holy Church, though he repent at last,

'Tis true he may not enter this abode,

For thirty times as long as he hath pass'd

In harden'd sin, if the probation be   140

Not shorten'd by the prayers from earth address'd.

Behold what gladness thou canst give to me!

Therefore, I pray thee, to my Constance tell

How thou hast seen me, and of this decree;

For here, by prayers of those on earth we profit well."   145

CANTO IV.

Argument

Dante ascends the mountain with difficulty.—He recognises
  Belacqua, who on earth was noted for indolence and
  procrastination.

Were in the fulness of our heart's content,
Or 'mid the suffering of some sharpest pain,
The spirit wholly in the reon intent,

  Then can it to no other thought attain ;
And this disproves the error which believes
Soul above soul our nature doth contain.

  Thus when the mind some outward thing receives,
Which holds it fixedly by sight or sound,
The flight of time no longer it perceives ;

  Because one faculty within is found
That listens, and the rest all dormant lie,
For they are free, the other as if bound :

And of this true experience had I
A proof, when listening to the speaker there.
The sun had risen full fifty grades on high,

  Nor of its onward course was I aware,
Till, with one voice, to us those spirits said :
"Behold ! the place for which ye seek is here."

  More wide the opening that is often made
Among the vines, and closed with thorny bent,
By labouring peasant when the grape grows red,

  Than was the entrance to the steep ascent,
Which now my guide and I essay'd alone,
Because another way those pilgrims went.

  The foot of man to Noli may go down,
And climb St. Leo and Bismantua's height ;
But, sooth to say, here must I needs have flown,

  Borne on the pinions swift and strong for flight,
Of ardent longing, as I strove to keep
Still close to him who gave me hope and light.

  Between the broken rocks we climb'd the steep ;
The stony ramparts press'd on either side,
And I was fain on hands and knees to creep.

  When to the upper edge we came, and spied

The open plain, I said: " Now whither flies
Our way, my Master !" and he thus replied :

  " Come onward where the mountain doth arise
Before us ; follow in my footstep's place,
Till there appear to us some escort wise."

  Too distant for the human eye to trace
Was that far summit ; and the coast went down
More steep than line unto the central space

  From half the quadrant.   Weary did I moan :
" O gentle father, turn thee and behold ;
If thou dost stay not, I am left alone."

  " My son," he said, " to reach this spot be bold ;"
And pointed upward to a ledge that round
The mountain did its summit all enfold.

  So strong the impulse in his words I found,
That prone on earth I struggled, till at last
My feet were stay'd upon the rocky bound.

  And on the ridge we sat us down to rest,
Turn'd to the east, the point from which we came ;
For pleasant is the view of dangers past.

  First to the island shore I look'd , from thence,
Up to the sun I gazed, and saw that earth

From the left side was stricken by its flame.

   The Poet well perceived that I look'd forth,
Amazed to see the chariot of the light,
There where it stood between us and the north.

   Wherefore he said : " If the Twin Brethren, hight
Castor and Pollux, near yon mirror lay,
Which sheds on every side its radiance bright,

   Thou then shouldst see the zodiac's golden ray
Yet nearer to the north its circles throw,
If still it mov'd within its ancient way.

   How this may be, if thou art fain to know,
Within thy thought imagine Zion's hill,
To stand, respective of this mountain, so

   That both should have one sole horizon, still
With diverse hemispheres ; and thus the road,
Where Phaeton his chariot drove so ill,

   Is seen toward the north of this abode,
Toward the south of Palestine ; and how
This may be so to thee is clearly shon'd "

   I said : " My Master, never, until now,
Saw I so clearly as I here discern,
Even where my mind appear'd to fall too low,

That the mid circle of the sons supern,
By skill'd in starry lore equator hight,
Which ever stands 'twixt sun and wintry bourne,

Even for the cause thou sayest, in our sight
Lies to the north; while yet the Jews behold
Southwards the radiance of the heavenly light.

But, if it please thee, I would fain be told
How long our journey: for the hill so much
Ascendeth, that the eye may not be bold

To reach the summit." " Know, this mount is such,"
He then replied, " that still the toil doth seem
More easy, as a higher point we touch:

And when the pathway thou at length shalt deem
So pleasant, that thy course shall be as light
As sailing in a bark adown the stream,

Thou then shalt have attain'd the furthest height;
There may thy weary limbs repose at last:
I say no more; but this I know aright."

He ceased; we heard a voice that us addrest,
And said: " Before the steep ascent, perchance,
It well may be thou shalt have need of rest."

And at that voice's sound we turn'd our glance;

A mass of rock we saw at the left hand,
Unnoticed when at first we did advance.

  Thither we went; and there, as they who stand
In idle mood, I saw, beneath the shade,
Some who appear'd, in sooth, a listless band.   105

  And one who seem'd with weariness down-weigh'd,
Sat, and his arms upon his knees did lean,
And, bending low, his face between them laid.

  "Good Master, look," I said, "for he, I ween,
Weareth an aspect yet more negligent   110
Than if dull idlesse were his next of kin."

  Then he toward us look'd with eyes intent,
Turning his face upon his knees, and said:
"Thou who art able, try the steep ascent."

  And then I knew him; nor my steps were stay'd   115
By the quick anguish of my breathing, weak
With that sharp toil. Scarcely he raised his head,

  As we approach'd, but on this wise he spake:
"Hast thou remark'd the sun, whose car of light
From the left shoulder doth its pathway take?"   120

  The lazy gesture of this idle wight,
And curtness of his speech moved me to smile;

Then I began : " Belacqua, for thy plight
 I grieve no more , but tell me, why beguile
Vainly the time ?   An escort dost thou wait ?
Or lingerest as thou were wont erewhile ? "
 And he : " My brother, wherefore should my feet
Essay the height with such an eager haste ?
God's angel ever sitteth at the gate,
 And will not let me enter, till is past
As long a time as I have spent on earth,
(For I delay'd repentance to the last,)
 If prayers which from a holy heart have birth,
Come not unto mine aid : for know that none,
Save from a pardon'd soul, have any worth."
 And then the Poet rose, and pointed on
And said : " Arise, and let us go , for o'er
Our heads is shining now the noonday sun ,
 And dusky Twilight stealeth tow'rd Morocco's shore."

CANTO V.

Argument.

Those who have delayed repentance are seen waiting for admission into Purgatory — Among them are Buonconte di Montefeltro and Pia Tolomei.

DEPARTING from those shades, I strove to hold
Still the same path as did my trusty guide ;
When one, with finger pointing, said : " Behold !

What wondrous thing is this ?   At his left side,
No ray of sunshine on the path is found :
Meseemeth, yet in life he doth abide."

I turn'd my eyes toward the voice's sound,
And saw them look with wonder and amaze
At me, and at the shadow on the ground.

My Master said : " Why dost thou backward gaze,
With anxious mind, and linger in thy walk ?
What matters it to thee, whate'er he says ?

Follow thou me, and let the people talk :
Be stedfast as a tower, that doth not bend
Its stately summit to the tempest's shock.

For he is ever further from the end
He aims at, in whose mind thought grows on thought,
For one to crush another aye doth tend."

Saving "I come," I could not answer aught :
And as I spake, swift to my cheek there sprang
The hue that shows us fit for pardon sought.

And then came tow'rd us, where the rocks o'erhang,
A band of spirits, moving soft and slow ;
And "*Miserere*," verse by verse, they sang.

They saw the darkness on the path below,
(Because on me was stay'd the solar flame,)
And changed their song to a long startled "Oh !"

Then unto us, as messengers there came
Two of that band, and thus their speech began :
"Fain would we know, in truth, your state and name."

And thus my guide made answer : "Now ye can
Return to them who sent you here, and say,
'He whom ye look on is a living man.'

If, for his shadow they their footsteps stay,

As I suppose, enough be this reply;
The honour given, he will to them repay."

No meteor stars did e'er so quickly fly,
At evening hour, across the deep serene,
Or August clouds upon a sunset sky,

As those swift messengers return'd again;
And once again came tow'rd us with the rest,
Fleet, as unbridled horses they had been.

"See, they are many who come on in haste,"
The Poet said; "thee they will beg for grace:
Therefore to listen as we go is best."

"O soul who journeyest to the blessèd place,
With the same limbs which on thy natal day
Thou hadst, a little linger in thy pace,"

Thus they began, "and look on us, we pray;
If thou hast known us tell of us on earth:
Ah! why such haste! Ah! wherefore dost not stay!

We all by violence have been cast forth
From life, and we were sinners till the last;
And then the light of heavenly grace had birth,

And we, forgiving and repentant, pass'd
From life, in peace with God; who gives us now

The pain of longing for our promised rest."

    And I " Although I look with stedfast brow,
I know you not, but if to you doth please
Aught that I can, O souls redeem'd from woe,   60

    Tell me, and I will do it, by that peace,
Which, following in the footsteps of my guide,
I seek from world to world withouten cease."

    And one began . " In faith we do abide
That thou wouldst aid us, though by oath unbound ,   65
If by no higher power thy will be tied.

    And I, who speak before the rest around,
Beseech thee, when the land thou shalt behold
That lies 'twixt Naples and Romagnan ground,

    Do not thy gentle courtesy withhold ;   70
But beg of those in Fano that they pray
To free me from the sins that me enfold.

    Thence was I ; but the wounds whence gush'd away
The blood where I abode, to me were dealt
Within Antenor's land ; even where I lay,   75

    Deeming myself most safe : the murd'rous guilt
Be unto him of Este ; for his wrath,
More fierce than righteous, hath that life-blood spilt.

But had I taken my flight by Mira's path,
When I my foes at Oriaco met,
Still were I in the land of living breath.

Unto the marsh I fled; and hard beset,
Entangled fell, amid the reeds and mire;
And earth was with my veins' dark river wet."

Then said another: " As thou dost aspire
To reach the summit of the lofty mount,
Aid me too to fulfil my just desire.

Buonconte, son of Montefeltro's Count,
Am I; by wife and friends am I forgot:
Therefore I ever walk with bended front."

And I to him : " Now tell me what sad lot,
So far from Campaldino, hath been thine,
That of thy sepulchre man knoweth not."

He said : " Mid Casentino's groves of pine,
The streamlet Archiano flows amain,
Above the Convent born, in Apennine.

There where its early name becometh vain,
Did I arrive, deep wounded in the throat;
Flying on foot, and 'sanguining the plain.

My eyes grew dim, and my last spoken thought

Was the sweet name of Mary: and I fell;
My corpse alone remain'd upon that spot.

I speak the truth, which thou again must tell:
As I sank down, an angel came from God,
To take me to Himself; and He of Hell

Cried out: 'Why dost thou me defraud!
Thou robb'st me only for one little tear:
Thou hast his soul, mine be the lifeless sod.'

Thou knowest well how gathers in the air
The humid vapour which descends in rain,
When risen unto a region cold and rare.

The evil Will that ever would attain
To evil, roused the dusky storm-wind's might,
By the dread power his nature doth contain.

And thus the valley, in the fading light
Of eve, was folded in a darksome veil,
From Pratomagno to the furthest height:

So that the heavy air came down in hail,
And rushing water, till the burden'd ground
Gave back the rain in streams; nor did they fail

To join the mountain torrents, which rebound
From rock to rock, toward the royal flood,

So wild, that nought to stay their course is found.
  My body, lying in its frozen blood,
The Archiano caught, and swiftly bore
Into the Arno; with its violence rude
  Loosing the sign of Holy Cross I wore,
Made on my breast in the last closing strife:
Then with its prey enwrapp'd me o'er and o'er."

  "Ah! when thou shalt return again to life,
And from thy weary journey hast repose,"
Thus spake a third, in tones with sorrow rife,

  "See that thou then forget not Pia's woes:
Sienna was my birthplace, and I died
In the Maremma: and this well he knows
  Who me, already widow'd, took to be his bride."

CANTO VI.

Argument.

Sardello.—Invective of Dante against the divisions of Italy, and
the government of Florence.

WHEN from a game of dice away they turn,
He who hath been the loser stays behind,
Repeats the throws, and sorrowful doth learn:

And with the winner all the crowd ye find;
Some after, some before, they strive, that he
Their suit won'd still be pleased to bear in mind.

He does not stay to hear what each may be;
But gives and listens as he goes along:
And he who hath received then leaves him free.

Even so was I, in this tumultuous throng,
Turning to them, now here, now there, my face,
And promising to aid them with my song,

There, came the Aretino with swift pace,
Even he who was by Ghin di Tacco slain ;
And he who drown'd in running from the chase :

And there, entreated me with humble mien
The younger Frederick ; and the Pisan knight
Who show'd the good Marzucco strong in pain.

I saw Count Orso ; there, too, met my sight
The soul who from its body was driven forth
(And for no crime) by malice and despite.

Of Peter de la Brosse I speak . on earth,
'Twere well the Lady of Brabant provide,
Lest she be in a flock of keener worth.

And now, as I was free on every side
From all those shades, who begg'd, with earnest cry,
For prayers of those on earth, to give them aid,

I thus began : " It seems thou dost deny,
O my Enlightener, somewhere in thy lay,
That prayers can bend the counsel of the sky ;

And yet for this alone those people pray.
Then tell me, shall their hope be all in vain ?
Or know I not aright what thou wouldst say ?"

And he to me , " What I have writ is plain ;

And these are led by no fallacious hope ;
If well thou lookest with thy reason sane.

Justice descends not from its mountain top ;
For in one moment love fulfilleth all
That stays the pilgrims from their journey's scope

And where I spake the words thou dost recal,
The prayer was answer'd not by heavenly ruth ;
Because disjoin'd from God its words did fall.

But still too lofty are those thoughts in sooth
For thee, until a teacher shall descend,
To be thy light 'twixt intellect and truth.

It well may be thou dost not comprehend :
I speak of Beatrice, whom thou at last
Shalt see all radiant on this mountain stand"

And I : "Good Master, come with greater haste ;
For now in truth I wish not for repose :
See how the shadow lengthens from the west."

" We shall go onward, while the daylight glows,
Far as we may," he answer'd ; "but yet
The fact is other than thou dost suppose.

He who behind yon mountain-peak doth set
Shall turn again, ere we the summit gain ;

Now by thy form no more his rays are let.

But there, behold a spirit who doth strain
His eyes toward us ; he will tell us how
Most quickly we the summit may attain."

We came to him : Oh ! what a lofty brow,
Thou Lombard soul, did thy great mind disclose,
And in thy gaze what grandeur grave and slow !

And with no word did he his lips unclose ;
But only look'd at us with steadfast eye,
Even as a lion couching in repose.

Yet Virgil still drew near to him, to try,
If he might lead us by an easier way :
To his demand the Shade made no reply ;

But of our life, and where our country lay
He question'd us.   And thus my guide began :
" Mantua "—the spirit, ere he more could say,

Sprang toward him from his place, " O Mantuan,
I am Sordello of thy land ;" and now,
As brothers, each unto the other clung.

Alas ! poor Italy, the home of woe,
Ship without pilot in an ocean wild,
No gentle lady, but a harlot thou !

So eager was that courteous spirit mild,
Only for the sweet sound of his own land,   80
To welcome joyfully his country's child :

And now in thee, not without warfare stand
Those who are yet alive ; and each gnaws each,
Of those whom but one wall and ditch defend.

Seek, wretched one, around thy circling beach :   85
Then turn thine eyes ; within thy bosom gaze ;
And see if anywhere sweet peace doth reach.

What boots it that on thee Justinian lays
The bridle, if the saddle be not fill'd ?
Else were there less of shame and sad amaze.   90

Ah ! ye whose mad dissensions should be still'd
In loyal obedience unto Cæsar's throne,
If thou wouldst understand what God hath will'd,

See how this beast is fierce and savage grown,
Because she is not govern'd by the spur,   95
And ye would rule her with the bit alone.

O German Albert, who forsakest her
Who all untamed and lawless has become,
While thou to ride this steed thy limbs shouldst stir,

On thee and on thy race may righteous doom   100

Fall from on high, made clearly manifest,
That he may fear who cometh in thy room.

Thou and thy father were in such hot haste
For distant conquest, that ye now permit
The garden of the empire to be waste.

Come look on Montague and Capulet,
Monaldi, Filippeschi, heartless power!
And some do groan, some only fear as yet.

Come, cruel, come, and thou shalt see how sore
The pains and sorrows by thy vassals borne;
And look how safe it is in Santaffior'

Come and behold thy Rome, who now doth mourn,
Lonely and widow'd; day and night she cries,
" My Caesar, wherefore leav'st thou me forlorn?"

Come see what love among thy people has;
And if nought else can thee to pity move,
At the dishonour of thy name arise!

And (be it said with reverence) God of love,
Who upon earth for us was crucified,
Dost fix thine eyes but on the realms above!

Or does there in thy counsels' depths abide
Some purpose for our good, by us unknown,

And lying from our vision all too wide?

For the whole land of Italy doth groan
Beneath the sway of tyrants; peasants swell
With pride, as though Marcellus were each one.

Rejoice, my Florence! those who in thee dwell,
To them do none of my reproaches reach;
Thanks to thy people, who provide so well!

Many are just of heart, but slow of speech,
Because they would take counsel of their thought,
Justice with thee springs from the tongue of each.

Many refuse the cares of state; unsought
Thy people eagerly reply and say:
"Behold, to me be all the burden brought."

Let them be glad, in sooth, for well they may,
For thou art rich, and wise, nor art afraid
Of any danger: is't not so, I pray?

Athens and Lacedæmon, they who made
The ancient laws, and were so deeply wise,
Have now their glories thrown into the shade

By thee who dost so subtilly advise,
That half November passes ere is done
That which thou in October didst devise;

How often in the time which late hath run,
Thy laws, thy dignities, thy coinage, thou
Hast changed, and eke thy citizens, each one !
    Remember this , and then bethink thee how
Thou dost resemble one in grievous pain,
Who on her couch no rest or ease may know ;
    Therefore to seek relief in change of place is fain.

CANTO VII.

—

AFTER the warm embrace of welcome glad
Had been repeated more than twice or thrice,
Sordell drew back, and "Who are ye?" he said.

"Ere to this mount the spirits might arise,
Worthy the paradise of God to win,
Octavius laid my corpse where now it lies ;

For I am Virgil , and no other sin
But lack of faith hath lost me heavenly bliss :"
Thus did my leader his reply begin.

As one who sees some wond'rous thing, I wis,
And knows not where he may his credence place,
But first he says, it is not ; then, it is ;

Sordello thus appear'd, and bow'd his face.

Again toward my guide he turn'd, the while
He spake, and humbly did his knees embrace :

"O glory of the Latins ! thou whose toil
The power of our old language hath made known,
Eternal honour of my native soil !

What grace or merit thee to me hath shown !
But if thou deignest to speak, then tell me now,
If thou hast come from Hell, and through what zone."

"Through all the circles of the realm of woe
Have I come hither," thus he made reply ;
"By strength from Heaven impell'd, I come and go.

Not deeds, but lack of deeds, has caused that I
May never see the Sun thou dost desire ;
And which by me was known too tardily.

There is a place below, not plagued with fire,
But only sad with darkness, where they mourn
With sighs alone, and not with wailings dire ;

There dwell I with the stainless babes new born,
The unbaptised, who have been slain by Death
Ere they our human guiltiness have worn.

And there I dwell with those who hope, nor faith,
Nor love have known ; yet without other sin

Still stedfastly have walk'd in virtue's path :

But, couldst thou aid us, gladly would I win
Some knowledge how to climb the mountain side,
Where Purgatory truly doth begin."

"There is no certain path," the Shade replied ;
"I am permitted all around to stray ;
Far as I can, I now will be your guide.

But see already how declines the day :
Ascend by night we may not ; thus 'tis well
To look for a fair sojourn while we may.

Far at our right a band of spirits dwell ;
There will I lead thee, if thou dost consent,
And who thou art, to them will gladly tell."

"But how is this !" was answer'd, "if intent
To climb this rock by night, is there some bar,
Or lack of strength that hinders the ascent ?"

The good Sordello bent him down, and there
Traced with his finger on the ground, and said :
"Thou canst not cross this bound'ry, while the star

Of day is hid from us ; and yet is laid
On thee no hindrance save the clouds of night :
Only the darkness makes thy will afraid.

Thus it might be, thou'dst turn thee from the height,
And wander downwards where the valley lies,
While the horizon hides the sunny light."

And then my Master, even as in surprise,
Made answer : " Lead us on, where thou hast said
It shall be well till day again arise."

But little further onward had we sped,
When I perceived that in the mount there lay
A vale like those of earth.   Then he who led

  Our footsteps spake : " Now thither is our way ;
Even where the coast the deepest hollow hath :
There may we wait the dawning of the day."

'Twixt smooth and rugged, by a winding path,
Did we toward that quiet valley go,
Where most its stony rampart 'minisheth.

Silver, and gold, and newly fallen snow ;
The shining wood of India ; Tyrian dye ;
The fresh-cut emerald and ruby's glow ;

If placed anear the leaves and blooms that vie
Within that dell, and all the ground bestrew,
In sooth, all dull and colourless would lie.

Nor was there only every lovely hue ;

The sweetness of a thousand scents, I ween,
Was mingled, floating on the evening dew.

"*Salve Regina,*" on the flowery green,
The spirits sat and sang : those souls whom yet
Beyond the valley's bound I had not seen.

" Before the dying sun hath fully set,"
Thus spake the Troubadour, our Mantuan guide,
" I would not that those spirits ye should greet.

Their looks and actions better may be spied
Here where the rock impendeth, than along
The path within the valley by their side.

He who is seated highest in the throng,
But, sad with thoughts of worthy deeds undone,
.Moves not his lips to join the others' song,

Was erst the Emperor Rudolph ; who alone
Could heal the wounds that Italy have slain ·
Slowly by others must the work be done.

He who to give him comfort seemeth fain,
Ruled in the land from whence the streams gush forth,
First Moldowa, then Elbe, towards the main :

His name was Ottocar ; of greater worth,
From youth, than Wincedaus his son ; even he

Who dwells in idle luxury on earth.

And he who in close counsel seems to be
With one of gentle aspect, as he fled
He died, dishonouring the fleur-de-lis

Look how he beats his breast By grief downweigh'd,
Behold the other, as in mournful trance,
Upon his palm he rests his weary head :

Father and kinsman of the curse of France
Are they ; his foul and wicked life they know,
And therefore grief doth pierce them as a lance.

And he who such a stalwart frame doth show,
And him of manly features joins in song,
Girt with the cord of valour erst did go.

If to the youth behind him in the throng
The sceptre of his kingdom had remain'd,
Virtue from sire to son had pass'd along.

It is not thus with those who since have reign'd ;
Frederick and Giacopo possess the land,
But of the better part have nought retain'd.

Full rarely through the branches doth ascend
The worth of human virtue ; thus He wills
Who gives it, that to Him all praise may tend.

And not yon Shade alone my speech fulfils ;
He also proves it who with him doth sing :
Thus Pugha and Provence have many ills.

For so much weaker do his branches spring,
As much as Constance boasts more joy, as wife,
Than Beatrice and Margaret's fate may bring.

And there behold the king of simple life,
Henry of England, sitting all alone :
His offshoots more with virtuous deeds are rife.

And in a lower place, to thee is shown
The Marquis William, aye with upward gaze .
For him and Alexandria they groan

Even now, in Monferrato and the Canavese

CANTO VIII.

Argument.

The evening hour.—Two angels chase away the serpent — Conrado Malaspina.

Now was the hour that hath the softest spell,

To turn the sailor's heart on homeward way,

When he that morn hath bade his friends farewell,

   And on the pilgrim saddest thoughts doth lay

Of love, whene'er he heareth from afar

The bell that seems to weep the dying day.

   Then I began to have no further care

Of hearing, as I look'd with eager eye

At one who raised his hands as if in prayer;

   Fixing his gaze upon the orient sky,

As saying unto God: "For aught but thee

I have no thought." And then his voice on high

He lifted up in softest melody,
Singing "*Te lucis ante*," in a strain
So sweet, it was bewilderment to me.

And all the rest, with pure and humble mien,
Still follow'd him throughout the holy hymn,
Raising their eyes unto the starry train.

Now, reader, see that well thou mark my theme,
Because so fine and subtle is the veil,
That, sooth to say, the vision is not dim.

The while this noble army did not fail
All silently to gaze toward the sky,
With look of expectation meek and pale,

From heaven I saw two holy angels fly;
By each of them a flaming sword was worn,
But pointless were those weapons from on high.

Green as the summer leaflets newly born
Their garments wore, that, struck by emerald wings,
Waved in a track of verdure all unshorn.

The one unto the height above us springs;
The other floated swiftly through the air,
Unto the rampart that the vale enringa.

I saw the gleaming of their golden hair;

But on their brows each glory did abide,
My mortal vision might not linger there.

"Know, both those angels come from Mary's side,"
Sordello said, "and they the valley hold
Safe from the snake that hither soon will glide.

And I who knew not where I might behold
The serpent, turn'd me to my faithful friend;
For terror chill'd my blood with shuddering cold.

And thus Sordello: "Now let us descend
Among the shadows of the royal dead;
To you they will a gracious welcome lead."

Only three steps, methought, I downward sped,
And in the valley was to me reveal'd
One, whom desire to look on me had led.

The gloom of evening all the air had fill'd;
Yet not so dark but 'twixt his eyes and mine
Was seen what at the first had been conceal'd.

And each toward the other did incline:
Gentle Judge Nino, I rejoiced for thee
That the accursed fate was none of thine!

Nor were there wanting words of courtesy;
And then he ask'd: "How long a time has fled

Since thou hast come across the distant sea ?"

I answer'd : " Through the chambers of the dead,
This morn I came, yet breathing earthly life,
Though seeking the unearthly am I led."

And as they listen'd to my answer brief,
He and Sordello started, even as one
Whose mind with sudden questioning is rife.

To Virgil then drew near the Mantuan ;
The other turn'd, and cried : " Up, Conrad, rise !
And see what by the grace of God is done."

And then to me : " By the great debt that lies
On thee, of thanks to Him who thus doth hide
His secret springs of action from our eyes,

When thou shalt be beyond the waters wide,
Bid my Joanna that her prayers may soar
There where the guiltless ne'er in vain have cried.

I think her mother loves me now no more,
Since she has laid aside her mourning veil ;
Tho' which perchance she would that still she wore.

In her it may be seen how soon doth fail
The faith of woman when the life is fled,
And the dead love is a forgotten tale.

For her, in sooth, Gallura's bard hath made
A statelier show above her sepulchre,
Than Milan's snake, which shall be o'er her laid."

He spake, and on his forehead did he bear
The aspect and the seal of righteous wrath,
As in due measure gentlest hearts may wear.

My eyes still wander'd on the heavenward path,
Even where the starry orbs most slowly turn,
As near its pole the wheel least motion hath.

Then Virgil thus : "My son, what wouldst thou
          learn ?"

And I to him : "At those three stars I gaze,
With whose resplendence all the sky doth burn."

He answer'd : "These have risen to fill the place
Of the four radiant planets thou hast seen,
Shedding this morn the glory of their rays."

Even as he spake, Sordell, with anxious mien,
Drew him unto himself and said, " Behold !
There comes our wicked enemy, I ween."

And where no circling rocks the vale enfold
A snake was gliding, clad in glistering mail,
Perchance like him who tempted Eve, of old.

Among the flowers there came the evil trail,
And as it turn'd, its tongue it darted, even
As doth a beast that licks itself.   To tell

How moved the pinions of the birds of heaven,
I have no power: I did but see they flow,
Cleaving the air; to me no more was given.

The rushing of those wings of emerald hue
Startled the serpent, and he swiftly fled;
Back to their posts the angels turn'd anew.

The Shade who at Judge Nino's call had sped,
Throughout the combat ever fixedly
Upon my form his eager gaze had stay'd.

"If for the lamp that leads thee thus on high,
Thou in thy will such oil wouldst find, as well
May guide thee to the heights of azure sky,"

Thus he began; "if thou of those who dwell
In Valdimagra hear'st true words of fame,
To me, who there was great, thy knowledge tell

For Conrad Malaspina was my name;
I was the younger of that ancient band;
And here I love my friends with purer flame."

I answer'd: "Never yet within your land

Was I; but where, in sooth, are any found,
Who know you not, throughout all Europe's strand?

The glory that your noble house hath crown'd,
Such fame doth give its lords and their domain,
He who ne'er yet was there, your praise may sound.

And as I would my journey's scope attain,
I swear your honour'd race still bears the prize
Of wealth, and power, and deeds of valorous men.

On them such grace of Art and Nature lies,
They, though a wicked Head the world doth twist
To sin, alone the evil path despise."

" Not seven times shall the sun have gone to rest,"
Thus did he answer, " in the bed which now
The Ram hath wholly cover'd and possest,

Till thy opinion, erst so courteous, grow
Fixed in thy brain, with stronger fastenings stay'd,
Than the report of other men may show,

If in its onward course God's will be not delay'd."

CANTO IX.

Argument.

As dawn, while Dante dreams that he is borne upwards by an eagle, he is carried by Lucia to the gate of Purgatory. — He enters to the sound of *Te Deum laudamus.*

Now Tithon's mistress, famed in ancient song,

On the far orient sky shed silver light,

As from her lover's arms she pass'd along:

   Her brow with starry diamonds was bright,

In figure of the creature swift and cold,

That with its tail strikes, darting in quick flight ;

   And twice the footsteps of the Night were told,

The steps which slowly ever onward pace ;

Downward the third its dusky wings did fold,

   When I, who breathed the breath of Adam's race,

Oppress'd with slumber laid me down among

·Our band of five, in that still, flowery place.

And in the hour when first her mournful song
The swallow sings before the sun doth shine,
Perhaps in memory of her ancient wrong;

And when our pilgrim fancies most incline
To lofty thoughts, and least to earthly theme,
And in their vision almost are divine;

Methought I saw above me, in my dream,
A golden plumaged eagle in the sky,
Who with spread wings intent to swoop did seem:

Above Mount Ida he appear'd to fly,
Where Ganymede's departing words were heard,
When borne to the consistory on high.

I thought within myself: "Perchance yon bird
Aids only those who from this hill aspire;
Nor for the living are his pinions stirr'd."

Then swooping round in many a circling gyre,
Swift as the dreadful thunderbolt he came,
And bore me upward to the sphere of fire;

And then it seem'd both he and I in flame
Were burning, and in such fierce ardour glow'd,
That from my dream I woke. In ancient fame,

'Tis said no otherwise Achilles show'd,

Awaking, when he strain'd his gaze to learn
What undiscover'd land was his abode,

   What time from Cheiron unto Scyra borne,
(While sleeping in his mother's arms he lies,)
Ere from that isle the Greeks made him return ;

   Thus did I rouse myself, and from mine eyes,
The heavy slumber and the dream were gone,
And I grew pale with terror and surprise :

   Beside me was my comforter alone ;
My face was turn'd toward the island shore
And for two hours the morning sun had shone.

   Then said my Master : " Fear thou not so sore ;
In sooth, we have attain'd a goodly height ;
Slack not thy efforts now, but strive the more.

   The gate of Purgatory now in sight
Appears ; behold the ramparts round it drawn ;
Ye enter where they seem to disunite.

   For in the twilight that precedes the dawn,
The while thy soul asleep within thee lay,
Afar beneath upon the flowery lawn,

   A Lady came to us, and thus did say :
' I am Lucia, who this slumb'rer would

Bear upward with me on the heavenly way.'

   Sordello and the rest of gentle mood
Remain'd; and through the early daylight clear
She bore thee hither: I her steps pursued.

   At last she paused, but ere she placed thee here,
Her bright eyes show'd to me the open gate:
Then she did with thy slumber disappear."

   And like to him who still in doubt doth wait,
But changes into comfort all his dread,
Joyful in knowing truly of his state,

   Thus was I; and when he who ever led
My steps, perceived me calm and free of care,
Upward he moved and I behind him sped.

   Reader, thou seest well how I prepare
My strain with greater art; because the theme
Of which I sing is aye more bright and fair.

   As we went on, before me did it seem
As though the wall were broken; and when we
Drew nearer to the gateway's dazzling beam,

   I saw the door and the gradations three
Which led to it; I saw their diverse hue,
And one who kept the portal silently.

And when my eyes the place more clearly knew,
I saw him seated on the highest grade ;
His forehead such resplendent glory threw

  I might not look on him ; a naked blade
He bore, that glitter'd with the fiery glow,
And oft thereon in vain my glance was stay'd.

  He spake : "Reveal your purpose ere ye go ;
Where is your guide ? 'tis well ye should beware
That thus your coming do not work you woe."

  My Master said : "From out the heavenly air
A Lady came, and bade us to this height
Ascend, whence may the arduous path be tried."

  "And may that Lady lead your steps aright,"
The courteous guardian answer'd, "as ye pass ;
To climb our staircase now put forth your might."

  Thither we came : the first was a bright mass
Of snowy marble, polish'd clear and pure,
So that I saw myself as in a glass.

  The second was of dusky hue obscure ;
The stone appear'd all burnt and rough in grain,
And cleft, in form of cross, did aye endure.

  The last lay heavy on the former twain,

And seem'd to me of porphyry as bright
As blood that gushes forth from out a vein.

Above the highest step, within my sight,
There sat God's angel on the threshold-stone,
That seem'd a glittering diamond of light. 106

Up the three steps, with Virgil's help alone,
I gladly pass'd; and then he spake: " Entreat
With meekness, that the bar may be withdrawn."

Humbly I fell before the holy feet;
And begg'd for grace to open to me now; 110
But first three times upon my breast I beat.

He, with his sword, seven times upon my brow
Wrote the first letter of the Plague of Sin;
And bade that I to wash those wounds should go.

His garments were of ashen hue, I ween, 115
Even like the dust before the whirlwind roll'd;
Two keys of diverse sorts he wore within.

Silver the one; the other was of gold;
First with the white, then with the red he strove
To open; which I gladly did behold. 120

He said: " If either of those keys should prove
Unyielding, nor unto my hand give heed,

One step along the path ye cannot move.

More precious one ; the other hath more need
Of art, and of the skill which doth excel :
Because by it alone the bolt is freed.

From Peter I received them : it were well
With e'en too ready ease to grant this grace,
He said, if at my feet the pilgrims fell "

And then the gateway of the holy place
He open'd, saying : " Enter ; but beware ;
For he must forth who looks with backward gaze."

When on the hinges that the portal bear,
Slow turn'd with grating sound the sacred door,
Whose bolts their deep metallic voice declare,

Less harshly roar'd Tarpeia's gate of yore,
When good Metellus all in vain had found
Resistance, and the treasure was no more.

At the first note, intent I turn'd me round,
And then " *Te Deum* " did it seem to me
I heard in music mingled with the sound.

Even such an image it appear'd to be,
As when ye hear sweet voices sing ; and they
Joan with the organ's notes in melody :

And now the words are heard, and now they die away.

CANTO X.

Argument.

First circle of Purgatory.—Examples of humility, sculptured in the white marble rocks.—The proud, burthened with heavy stones, advance towards Dante and Virgil.

AFTER we pass'd the threshold of the gate,
The which our souls, from love of ill, disuse,
The ill that makes the crooked way seem straight,

  Sounding with heavy clang I heard it close:
Had I a backward glance toward it thrown,   5
What for my error had been fit excuse!

  Now we ascended through the fissured stone,
That fled and then advanced, on either part,
Like ocean billows, ever and anon.

  "In truth, we somewhat here have need of art,"   10
My guide began, "as through this cleft we go,
And now the walls jut forth, and now depart."

And thus we in our journey were so slow,
That, sinking once again unto its rest,
The darken'd border of the moon was low,

Ere through this needle's eye our steps had pass'd.
But when we, freed, throughout its toils had gone,
And issued to the open plain at last,

I being weary, and the way unknown
By either, there we rested, in a place
Than pathway through the wilderness more lone.

Here from its edge that borders empty space
Unto the rock ascending still on high,
The human body thrice its length might trace.

Far as my mortal sight had power to fly,
Now gazing to the left, and now to right,
The cornice seem'd the same unto mine eye.

Not yet our footsteps had essay'd the height,
And, as toward the rocky wall I turn'd,
I saw that of the purest marble white

It was: with loveliest sculptures all adorn'd;
So fair, they Polycletus put to shame,
And, by their side, e'en Nature's self were scorn'd

The angel who unto Judea came,

Bearing the message of long wept-for peace,

And oped the gate erst kept by swords of flame ;

  Upon that rock for aye he did not cease

Sculptur'd to stand in attitude so fair,

He seem'd no silent image. To increase

  The marvel, it appear'd as if he there

Said " Ave ," for anear him was pourtray'd

She who the key of heavenly love did bear

  And in her act it seem'd as though she said :

" Behold the handmaid of the Lord !" as plain

As impress of a seal on wax is made.

  " Do not thy mind entirely thus retain

Within one spot," then said my gentle guide,

Who near to me his steps did still detain.

  Thereat I turn'd my glance , and by the side

Of Mary's image, nigh to him who even

But now to rouse my 'mazed thoughts had tried,

  Another hist'ry in the rock was graven :

Wherefore I pass'd by Virgil, and drew near,

That to my sight more plain it might be given.

  Depicted there the cart and oxen bear

The Ark of God ; that we the dreadful fate

Of those who holy rites usurp should fear.

    A crowd was gather'd round, in festal state :
Divided in seven quires, unto mine eyes
They sang ; unto my ears did silent wait

    Even in such manner did the incense rise,
Carved within that fair imagining,
In me one sense said No, another Yea.

    Preceding those the holy vase who bring,
The dancers were by the meek Psalmist led,
Who on that day was more and less than king.

    And at a palace-window sculptured
Sat Michal, on the pageant looking down,
As doth a woman scornful and sad.

    I moved my steps a little further on,
That I another hist'ry might behold,
Next that of Michal, glittering in the stone.

    For in the sculpture was the glory told,
Of him who caus'd St. Gregory to seek
The vict'ry that the gate of Hell unroll'd.

    Of the good Emperor Trajan do I speak ;
There a poor widow seem'd, with mournful cry,
To grasp his steed, while tears flow'd down her cheek

Around, a gallant throng doth stand for aye,
Of arméd horsemen ; and above his head
The golden eagles rank themselves on high.

   Among the crowd it seem'd as though she said :
" Avenge me, Sire, avenge me of my woe,
On him who smote my son that he is dead."

   And he appear'd to answer : " Let me go ;
Wait thou till I return again."   She cried,
(As one whose grief in hastiness doth show,)

   " If thou returnest never !"   He replied :
" He who shall reign instead of me will see
Thee righted." • But she said : " Thou put'st aside

   Thy duty ; and what boots it unto thee
Another's virtue !" "Then be of good cheer,"
He answered ; " for thy cause full speedily,

   Ere I depart, shall be adjudged : I here,
By justice and by pity am delay'd."
Now He to whom there never doth appear

   That which before was hidden, clearly made
This speech seem visible unto our sight,
Now unto us, because not here portray'd.

   While on the sculptured meekness with delight

I gaz'd, because its beauty show'd the trace
Of Him whose mind imagin'd it aright,

  "Behold where many come, with tardy pace,"
The Poet whisper'd, "they to me will show
The way to climb unto the highest place."

  My eyes, that wand'ring all around did go,
(Because on each new thing they fain are stay'd,)
To turn again towards him were not slow.

  Reader, I would not thou shouldst be afraid
The path of penitential grief to try,
For hearing how God wills the debt be paid.

  Think not upon the suff'rings : let thine eye
Rest on the future : for when most severe,
They cannot pass into Eternity.

  Thus I began · "My Master, that which here
Advances, seems not human to my gaze ;
I know not what, so strange doth it appear."

  And he to me : "The heavy load which weighs
So sore, that they are to the earth opprest,
At first bewilder'd me in dire amaze.

  But if thine eyes thou stedfastly dost rest
On them who thus those pond'rous stones endure,

Thou see'st how each one crawls upon his breast "

O haughty Christians, miserable, poor !
Who in the darken'd vision of your mind,
Deem in the path of ill ye are secure ;

Do ye not know we are the insect kind,
Born the angelic butterfly to form,
That flies to justice where no screen ye find ?

Why does such swelling pride your souls deform ?
Ye are but beings of defective race,
Condemn'd to crawl for ever as a worm !

As, to sustain a cornice in its place,
Ye see a figure who, in crouching low,
Doth almost join his knees unto his face,

So that true sorrow from the feign'd woe
Is born within the gazer ; thus, when seen
Intently, did to me their semblance show.

And more or less they were bow'd down, I ween,
As they a less or greater burden bore ;
But he who had most patience in his mien,

Weeping, appear'd to say, " I can endure no more."

CANTO XI.

"FATHER, who hast thy dwelling place on high,
Not circumscribed, but that thou lovest more
Thy first-created of the empyreal sky,

  To hymn thy wondrous name let praises soar
From every creature, as 'tis meet and right
To render thanks unto thy glorious power.

  Send unto us thy heavenly kingdom bright;
For of ourselves we have no strength to gain
Its peace, although we strive with all our might.

  Even as thy holy angels aye are fain
To do thy will, while they Hosanna sing,
The selfsame sacrifice be done by men.

`And unto us our daily manna bring ;
Without it, as we pass this desert drear,
Backward we go, in all our journeying.

As we the ill that we have suffer'd here
Forgive, do thou forgive us, from the cry
Of our demerits turn away thine ear.

Our feeble strength do not so sorely try
With our dread ancient Enemy ; but free
Our souls from him who fain would make us die.

Not for ourselves this prayer, O Lord ; for we
Of and against temptation have no need :
For those who yet are living let it be "

Thus, begging for themselves and us good speed,
They toil'd beneath their burden ; even as they
Who from an evil dream would fain be freed.

'Neath the unequal load that on them lay,
Up the first cornice wearily they went,
Purging the darkness of the world away.

If to our help their prayers are heavenward bent,
For them what should we do, in whom doth he
The root from whence a chasten'd will is sent.

We ought to aid them, sooth, to purify

Their souls from earth; that, gladsome and secure,
They may ascend unto the starry sky.

"As from the heavy load which ye endure,
Ye would be early freed, and on the wings
Of swift desire attain joy's fountain pure,

I pray you, show to us the way that brings
Most quickly to the staircase which we seek,
And where the path least steep and dangerous springs

For he who with me climbs this mountain-peak,
Because he breathes the breath of Adam's race,
Against his will his mortal flesh is weak."

Thus he who led me by those arduous ways,
They answer'd; and I noted not aright
By whom the words were said, or from what place;

But one thus spake. "Now turn ye to the right,
And journey by our side, unto the pass
Of possible ascent for living wight.

Were I not hinder'd by the heavy mass
That downward ever weighs my haughty head,
And nails my eyes to earth, with sad harass,

This living one, whose name thou hast not said,
I'd look upon, to know him, and inspire

His pity for the grief upon me laid.

   I was of Latium , and my Tuscan sire
Guglielmo Aldobrandeschi : his high praise
Perchance ye have not heard ? The deeds of fire,

   And ancient blood of my ancestral race,
Within me did such thoughts of pride impel
(Forgetful of the common stock and place

   From which we spring) that my proud glances fell
On all men with contempt ; and thence I died,
And Campagnatico doth know it well.

   Humbert my name : and not alone did pride
Do ill to me, but unto all I led,
Who 'gainst Sienna were with me allied.

   And thus this burden on my weary head
I must endure, till God shall grant me grace :
What was undone when living, 'mong the dead

   I must fulfil." Listening, I bent my face ;
And one (not he who spoke) then turn'd him round,
Beneath the heavy load that sorely weighs ;

   And fix'd his eyes intently, till he found
Remembrance wake again : then call'd to me
Who journey'd with them, bending to the ground.

I said : "Can thou then Oderisi be,
The honour of Agobbio, and that Art
In Paris call'd *illumining* !"   Then he :

" Nay, Francis of Bologna did impart
More beauty to his pencillings, I ween :
To him be all the glory , mine, in part.

While yet on earth, in truth I had not been
So courteous in my speech ; for the great love
Of praise, on which my heart too much did lean.

Here of such pride the punishment I prove ,
And here I had not been ; but in the hour
Of his, I turn'd me unto God above.

Oh ! the vainglory of all human power !
How short a time its blossom doth endure,
If afterward the darkness do not lower !

For Cimabue doom'd himself secure,
Within the field of painting ; Giotto now
Hath caused the former fame to be obscure.

Thus from one Guido doth the glory go
Unto another, of the gift of song ;
And he, perchance, is born who will bring low

The pride of both.   The splendours that belong

Unto the fame of earth are but a wind,

That in the same direction lasts not long

  What more thy praise, if thou be consign'd

Unto the grave in fulness of thy days,

Than if thou left'st but childhood's hours behind,   105

  Ere pass a thousand years? A shorter space,

To the long ages of Eternity,

Than an eye's flash, unto the orbit's mass

  That slowest moves along the starry sky.

All Tuscany resounded with the fame   110

Of him who doth so slow the pathway try:

  Now in Sienna scarce ye hear his name,

Even where he was the Master, in the hour

That the proud mob of Florence put to shame.

  All your renown is like the summer flower,   115

That blooms and dies ; because the sunny glow,

Which brings it forth, soon slays with parching power."

  And I to him : " The truth thy speech doth show,

Within my heart reproves the swelling pride ;

But who is he of whom thou spak'st but now ?"   120

  " Provenzan de' Salvani," he replied ,

" And he is here for his presumptuous heart,

Because to sway Sienna once he tried

Since he did from his mortal life depart,
Thus he has gone, unresting; such the debt
They pay who act on earth too bold a part."

And I "If it be true, that they who wait
Until the close of life ere they repent,
Must stay beneath, and here ascend not yet,

(If to their aid no holy prayers be sent)
As long a time as was their earthly life,
Why for his sake did justice now relent?"

"When his career with glory was most rife,"
He answer'd, "freely in Sienna's street,
Although he felt in every vein the strife,

Begging for alms he humbly did entreat
For him, his friend, who in the dungeon-cell
Of Charles was held in durance Now 'tis meet

I say no more the thing which thus I tell
Perchance is dark; but little time shall speed,
Before thy neighbours make thee know it well:

For him, free entrance here was won by that good
    deed

CANTO XII

Argument

Dante observes, sculptured on the pavement, instances of pride
and its punishment.—An Angel meets him, and, conducting
him to the second circle, effaces the first of the seven
letters from his brow.

TOGETHER, even as oxen in the yoke,
Beside that burden'd spirit, bending low
I went, until my gentle Master spoke:

"Leave him, and on thy journey speed; for know,
Here it is good the sail and oars be strain'd,
That swiftly on its course thy bark may go."

As one who would press onward I regain'd
At once my stature's fullest height, though still
Low in humility my thoughts remain'd.

And in my Master's steps, with ready will
I follow'd eagerly, as he and I
Sprung lightly up to climb the arduous hill.

When thus he said : " Now downward turn thine eye ;
It shall be well for thee to cheer thy way,
With sight of that whereon thy footsteps be."

As, lest the memory should pass away
Of those who in the sepulchre are laid,
The name they bore, when in the land of day,

Is written on their tomb ; and thence the dead
Remembrances awake, and once again
Flow forth the tears that gentle spirits shed :

Thus did I see, but lovelier, I ween,
The sculptured forms our rock-hewn pathway bore ;
For out by loftier artist it had been.

And him I saw, who noblest aspect wore,
Of all created beings, from the sky
Like lightning downward hurl'd for evermore.

And there I saw the great Briareus die,
Pierced by celestial arrow ; in my sight,
Cold in the chill of death he seem'd to lie.

And Mars, and Pallas, and the Lord of light,
Still arm'd around their father stood, and gazed
On the dead giants slaughter'd in the fight.

Nimrod, beneath the mighty work he raised,

Look'd upon them who erst in Shinar's plain
Were with him, all bewilder'd and amazed.

O Niobe, with what a mournful mien
Thy sculptured image on the path I knew,
'Twixt seven and seven of thy loved children slain '

O Saul, who seem'd as though thy weapon slew
Its master, even as on Gilboa's hill,
Which from that hour hath felt nor rain nor dew !

O mad Arachne, there I saw thee still,
To spider half transform'd, upon the thread
Which thou, in spinning, work'dst for thine own ill '

O Rehoboam, now thy semblance shed
No menacing, but through a city's gate,
Hotly pursued, thy chariot swiftly fled '

And still the lifeless pavement did relate
How erst Alcmaeon paid, in vengeance dire,
The gems his mother won for evil fate.

It told the tale, how, in unfilial ire,
Sennacherib by his own sons was kill'd,
Who in the temple left their murder'd sire.

The deed of cruel fierceness was reveal'd,
Done when Tamyris unto Cyrus said :

" For blood thou thirsted'st, now with blood be fill'd."
  And there the army of Assyria fled,
When Holofernes met his death of woe,
And there I saw the relics of the dead

  And Troy in dust and wilderness lay low;
O Ilion, how thou wert all mean and vile,
Traced in the picture which thy fate did show !

  Who was the master of the pen or style,
That to those shadowy forms had power to give
The life which seem'd to move and breathe, the while ?

  The dead were dead; the living seem'd to live :
Nor truth itself a truer semblance hath,
Than what I bending trod.   O sons of Eve,

  On earth ye walk in haughtiness and wrath,
Erect, with brow uplifted as in pride,
Nor bend that ye may see your evil path !

  Our footsteps turn'd along the circuit wide,
Around the mountain ; and the day was spent,
More than by unfreed thought might be descried,

  When he who heedfully before me went
Began : " Now raise thy head ; no longer may
Thine eyes so wholly on the path be bent.

Behold a heavenly angel on his way
Toward us ; and again the footsteps turn,
Of the sixth maiden in the band of day.

  With reverence thy looks and acts adorn,
And thus to aid us upward he may choose ;
Think that this day can never more return."

  My Master, sooth to say, did often use
To chide, and say : " Thy steps too ling'ring are ;"
And here I now his meaning might not lose.

  Then came that lovely Being from afar,
Clothed in white robes, and bearing on his brow
The trembling glory of the morning star.

  On outspread wings he floated ; and he now
His arms extended tow'rds us, as he spake :
"Behold the steps where ye with ease may go.

  Few, few there are who will this pathway take ,
O mortals, born to soar unto the skies,
Why doth so little wind your pinions break ?"

  He led us where a rugged entrance lies ;
And then he swept my forehead with his wing,
And bade me to ascend in fearless guise.

  As when ye try the arduous heights which bring

Your steps unto the church that looks adown,
Where Rubaconte o'er the flood doth fling

His arch, amid the nobly guided town,
Yet for the staircase, made in olden days,
When fraud in court or cask was all unknown,

More easy; thus by gentler-sloping ways,
The pilgrim climbs unto the higher bourne;
Yet him on either side the stone doth graze.

And as we hither did our footsteps turn,
"*Beati pauperes spiritu*" we heard,
Melodious more than ye on earth may learn.

Ah! how unlike these portal gates appear'd,
To those of Hell; ye enter here with song,
And there with lamentations wild and weird.

And now we pass'd the sacred stair along;
And more, meseem'd, than erst upon the plain,
To climb the summit I was light and strong.

Then I: "My Master, say, what weight hath lain
On me so sore, from which I now am free,
That scarcely do I feel fatigue or pain?"

He answer'd: "When the seven times written P;
The sign of sin, imprinted on thy brow,

As one is blotted out, shall wholly flee,

   Then from thy forward will such strength shall flow,

Thy limbs no longer weariness must bear,

But in the steep ascent delight shall know."

   And then I did as one who still doth wear

Some strange thing on his brow, nor doth he wot

Thereof, until he sees the people stare;

   And as, to search it out, his hand is brought,

And seeks, and finds, and doth fulfil the quest,

Of which his eye, in sooth, perceiveth nought:

   Thus, with my fingers wide outspread, I traced

But six the letters that my brow defiled,

Erst by the guardian of the keys imprest;

   And, looking at me now, my gentle Leader smiled.

CANTO XIII

Second circle, where Envy is punished

Now we had gain'd the summit of the stair,
Where for the second time recedes that hill,
Which from the pilgrim all his sins doth bear.

And here, as at the first, a cornice still
Encircles all the mountain ; but I know
Its arc more quickly did the circuit fill.

No sign, or form of sculpture met my view ;
But on the bank, and on the level way,
The stone was of a dull and livid hue.

" If here to ask the passengers we stay,"
The Poet reason'd thus, " I fear, perchance,
That all too long we may our choice delay."

Then turn'd he to the sun a stedfast glance ;
His right foot firm upon the ground he prest,
While circling round, his left he did advance,

And said : "O fairest Light, in whom I trust,
Lead thou us on, throughout this path unknown ,
For here we have much need of guidance just.

Thy golden splendours on the world are thrown ;
And if by lawful cause we are not stay'd,
Our steps should walk within thy rays alone."

As far upon our way we now had sped,
As on this lower earth were call'd a mile,
Swiftly, because by ardent longing led ;

And spirit voices, all unseen the while,
Came floating tow'rd us, on the viewless air,
Inviting us to feast on love's own smile

The first who did the gentle message bear
" *Venem non habent*" said , and aye this lay
Came from afar, in echoes sweet and clear.

Ere in the distance they had died away,
A voice " I am Orestes" said ; and still
Pass'd on, nor longer did with us delay.

" O father," then I said, " what voices fill

Mine ears ! " and as I spake, a third drew nigh,
Crying "Give love to him who does you ill."

Then my good Master : " In this zone they lie
Who for the guilt of envy suffer pain :
Thus love, for them, the knotted scourge doth tie.

Far different is the curb that must restrain
The evil will ; as thou shalt hear, ere we
Unto the pass of pardon can attain.

But look with stedfast gaze, and thou shalt see,
Before us, some who seated on the ground,
And ranged along the bank, all seem to be.

And then, with wond'ring eyes I look'd around,
And shadowy forms I saw, in mantles weird,
Of the dull colour of the stony bound.

When we were somewhat nearer, they appear'd
To cry : " O Mary, pray for us ," and then
To all the Saints their Litany we heard.

I think that none among the sons of men
Have hearts so hard, as, for those spirits' woe,
Who in this circle came within my ken,

To feel no pity. When I nearer saw
Their gestures, sorrowful compassion made

Tears from my eyes in floods to overflow.

   They in vile garb of sackcloth were array'd,
And each upon the other's shoulder leant,
And on the stony bank they all were stay'd.

   Even so the blind, whose every store is spent,
Sit begging near the churches, and beseech
For alms, their heads upon each other bent :

   And thus, not only from their mournful speech,
Does pity wake in him who passes by ;
Not less their looks have power his heart to reach.

   And, as unto the blind the sunny sky
Brings no bright joy, those Shades I speak of now
Perceive no blessed radiance from on high ;

   For 'neath their brows, an iron thread did sew
The lids together, as a falcon's eyes
Ye close, when from his Master he would go.

   Meseem'd, it here were in discourteous guise
To pass, when seeing, yet of them unseen ;
Wherefore I turn'd me to my counsellor wise ;

   And well he knew what these my thoughts had been,
And thus he did not wait for my demand.
" Speak ; but thy words must here be few, I ween,"

He said ; and came to me, toward that bend
Where round the cornice no encircling wall
Between me and the precipice did stand.

Anear me, seated by the cliff, were all
The Shades, from whose fast-closèd lids there ran
The mournful drops which o'er their cheeks did fall.

Then I toward them turn'd, and thus began:
"O ye, who have the certain hope, one day
To see the Light which gladly ye had won,

As ye would grace should quickly wash away
The guilt from out your conscience, so that clear
And bright may there descend the heavenly ray,

Speak, (for to me the knowledge were most dear,)
If ye be Shades of Latium : it were well,
Perchance, that I might know if each be here."

" My brother, in a land that doth excel
We all have our true home , but thou wouldst say,
Who pilgrims erst in Italy did dwell."

A little farther onward in the way
Than where I stood, as of this voice I deem'd,
And to draw nour to it I did essay.
Among the rest, I saw a Shade who seem'd

To wait ; and wouldst thou ask me in what grass ?
As one on whom the sun hath never beam'd.

  "Spirit," I said, "who for the hope to rise
Dost suffer pain, I pray thee not to hide
Thy name, or where thine earthly dwelling has."

  "Sienna was my home," the Shade replied ;
"And, with the rest, I cleanse me from my blame,
Weeping to Him whose love is still our guide.

  No sapience had I, although my name
Was Sapia ; because another's tears
Even as a wish'd-for joy to me became :

  And, lest thou think I would deceive thine ears,
Be all my folly unto thee reveal'd.
As I went down into the vale of years,

  My citizens were met in Colle's field,
Against their enemies ; then did I pray
To God for that which he indeed had will'd.

  There in the battle was their proud array
Turn'd to the bitterness of flight : and now,
Within my heart surpassing gladness lay ;

  So great, that daringly I raised my brow
To Heaven, and said : ' I fear thee never more ;'

As doth the bird when winter sunbeams glow.

    Though peace I sought with God ere life was o'er,

I had not yet had entrance to this place,   125

To purge away my guilt by penance sore,

    If, in his prayers before the throne of grace,

Pietro Pettignano had forgot

His pity for my sad and evil case.

    But who art thou who askest of our lot,   130

Walking among us with unclosèd eyes,

And living breath, if I deceive me not?"

    I said : " My lady, one day, shall on this who

Be closed, yet little time it shall be so,

For seldom have they look'd in envious guise   135

    Far greater is the terror which doth grow

In thought within me of the torment dread,

That weighs upon the burden'd souls below."

    And she to me . " Who hath thee hither led,

If back thou goest to the world beneath?"   140

" He who is with me, and no word hath said,"

    I answer'd ; "still unknown to me is death :

Then speak, if thou wouldst that for thee I bring,

O chosen one, the prayers of living breath?"

"This is, in sooth, so new and strange a thing," 145
She said, "It needs must be our Heavenly Sire
Doth hold thee in his love's o'ershadowing :

　Therefore, by all that thou dost most desire,
I beg thy prayers. If to the Tuscan land
Thou goest, tell that heavenward I aspire. 150

　Thou shalt behold my friends among the band
Who trust in Talamone ; hope more vain
Than e'en in seeking Dian's fount doth stand :

　But they who rule the fleet shall have most loss and
　　　pain.

CANTO XIV.

———

Guido del Duca inveighs against the inhabitants of the
Val d'Arno.

"Now who is this who wanders round our hill,
Ere yet the hand of death hath set him free,
And opes and shuts his eyes at his own will ? "

"Who he may be, I know not ; but to me
He seemeth not alone : more near art thou ;
That he may answer, greet him courteously."

Two spirits, on each other bending low,
Discours'd of me, as and they there reposed ;
Then, to accost me, raised each sightless brow ;

And one began : " O soul who, still enclosed
Within thy body, journeyest to the skies,
I pray that of thy favour be disclosed

Who thou mayst be, and whence.   Such wonder hes
Within us, at the grace God doth vouchsafe,
As from so strange a thing may will arise."

And I : " There is a Tuscan stream, whose wave
That hath its mountain source in Falterone,
More than a hundred miles of course doth crave ;

Anear it was I born : but to make known
My name, were but to speak in idle mood ;
Because, as yet, to fame it hath not grown."

" If I aright thy words have understood,"
Thus he who first accosted me replied :
" I think that now thou speak'st of Arno's flood."

The other said : " But wherefore doth he hide
The river's name, even as a man afraid
To speak of somewhat monstrous ! "   By his side,

The soul, to whom he spake, this answer made :
" In sooth, I know not ; but, perchance, 'tis well
That valley's name should never more be said.

For, mid the Alpine heights which most excel
In the rich store of founts, and whence is riven
Pelorus, do its early sources dwell ;

Thence to the spot where to the sea is given

What first the clouds receive from the salt tide
Which nourishes each stream, a Virtue driven,

And, like a serpent, chased from every side ;
Perchance for the ill fortune of the place,
Or for the evil men who there abide

So much is changed the nature of the race
Who dwell in that sad valley, that they seem
Like those whom Circe held in direful case.

In truth, of them as of foul swine I deem,
(More fit to feed on husks than human food,)
'Mong whom at first doth flow its scanty stream.

Next, it descends mid wretched curs, who would
Provoke a quarrel, with no power to fight,
And turns away from them, in scornful mood.

The river, hurrying onward in its flight,
Finds that the dogs to savage wolves have grown ;
Thus are its waters still in mournful plight.

And then by darker gulfs it rushes down,
And finds the foxes, with sharp cunning fil'd,
Where fear of any master is unknown.

And for no listener shall my speech be still'd ;
'Twere well that this man should remember aye

What a true spirit hath to me reveal'd.

  One of thy lineage, at no distant day,

Those wolves from the wild river's bank shall drive,

And with his fierceness sorely them affray :

  Their flesh will sell while they are yet alive,

And slaughter them like beasts , and thus on earth

Himself of fame and them of life deprive.

  Bloody, from the drear wood he issues forth,

And leaves it such, that for a thousand years

It shall not have again its early worth."

  As, at the warning voice of future fears,

The listener stops in sad and thoughtful mood,

Musing what form the coming danger wears,

  Even so, that other Shade who listening stood,

A mournful aspect bore upon his brow,

Soon as this prophecy he understood.

  Their words and looks made me desire to know

What might, on earth, their name and dwelling be ;

Thus soft entreaty from my lips did flow.

  He said, who first had spoken : " Now I see

Thou dost desire that unto thee I should

Be courteous more than thou wouldst be to me ;

But, since our Heavenly Sire hath thus endued
Thee with His grace, I will not say thee nay.
Guido del Duca am I; and my blood

Was so consumed by envy's livid ray,
That but to see a man with joyous face
Turn'd all my own to paleness dull and gray:

I reap what I have sown.   O human race,
Why do ye thus your very hearts entwine
With that wherein for consort is no place!

This is Riniero; of the ancient line
Of Calboli the glory and the pride:
None of his heirs do with his valour shine.

And not alone his kinsmen, who abode
Anear the Po, 'twixt Apennines and sea,
From the true good to folly turn aside;

Because the land is full of plants which be
So venomous, that all too late ye would
Strive from their poison-roots the ground to free.

Where are Manardi, Lizio the Good,
And Traversaro, and Carpigna now!
O Romagnuoli of ignoble blood!

When shall Bologna a new Fabbro show!

And Bernardin di Fosco in Faenza,
Where from small seed a noble stem did grow !
   Then, Tuscan, marvel not, although I chance
To weep at Guido della Prata's name,
And Ugolino d' Azzo, with us once ;   105

   Tignoso, and the band who with him came ;
The Anastagi, Traversara's race,
(Both, now alas ! unknown to virtue's fame,)

   And knights, and dames, and deeds of worthy praise,
And toil, inspired by love and courtesy,   110
Where now all hearts are sunk in evil ways ,

   O Brettinoro, wherefore dost not flee,
Since all thy noble rulers now have gone,
And many more, that they unstain'd may be !

   In sooth, 'tis well that heirs there should be none,   115
In Bagnacavallo ; and to bring forth seed
Conio and Castrocaro ill have done.

   Though, when their demon-father hence shall speed,
Pagani's sons may prosper ; yet the same,
For aye, the witness of each guilty deed.   120

   O Ugolin de' Fantoli, thy name
Is safe, for there are none to dim its light,

And stain, in after years, its noble fame.

But, Tuscan, leave me ; more I now delight
To weep, than hold discourse : for this our speech
Recalls again my country's mournful plight "

We knew the sound did to those spirits reach
Of our departing steps ; nor did they say
Aught that distrust of our new path might teach.

Now, as alone we wended on our way,
A voice, like crashing thunder, cleft the air :
" He who shall find me, surely will me slay,"

It said, and pass'd, as when the stormwinds bear
The heavy clouds afar ; even so, once more
Only the silence fell upon my ear

And then there came another voice, that wore
The self-same likeness of the angry moan
Which tracks the storm ; and these the words it bore

" I am Aglauros, who was turn'd to stone."
Then I drew near to him my steps who led,
And sought the shelter I had ever known

Already stillness through the air was shed,
And thus he spake : " Behold the curb of woe,
By which your course should aye be governed.

But yet ye take the bait your ancient foe
Holds out, that he may give a deadly wound ;
Thus little strength doth rein or bridle show.

Heaven calls you to itself, and, circling round,
Unfolds its light and loveliness etern ;
But ye still fix your eyes upon the ground

Thus are ye scourged by Him who doth all hearts
    discern."

CANTO XV.

Argument.

An Angel invites Dante and Virgil to continue the ascent.—
Theological questions concerning eternal beatitude.—Vision
of Dante.

As much as, 'twixt the third hour of the day
And dawn, appeareth of the heavenly sphere
Which ever moveth as a child at play,

There seem'd, as now the eventide drew near,
The same, ere yet the sun should sink to rest ;
The hour of vesper there, and midnight here.

Upon my brow the golden rays impress
Their seal, because we journey'd round the hill
In such a manner that we faced the west.

When I more blinding than at first did feel
The sudden splendour on my forehead weigh,
Amazed at what that glory might reveal,

I raised my hand, to screen me from the ray
Too pure and piercing in excess of light,
Which did my feeble vision so affray.

As, when from watery sheen or mirror bright,
The beams, refracted from the opposing part,
Spring back in equal manner to our sight,

And, as they fall, so much do they depart
From the straight line, in equal rule and guise,
As plainly show experience and art ;

Even thus it seem'd this wondrous light did rise,
And smote my brow as if with burning fire,
While swiftly sank to earth my blinded eyes.

I said : "What thing is this, O gentle sire,
From which my dazzled vision finds no shade,
As it draws nearer ?"   "Let it not inspire

Much marvel in thy thought," thus Virgil said,
" If yet the sons of Heaven are all too bright
To look on.   He is come to give thee aid :

And soon it will not pain thy mortal sight
To see such beings ; but with purer thought,
Thou mid celestial quires shalt find delight."

When near that Blessèd One our steps were brought,

He thus accosted us with joyous voice :
" Here mount a staircase with less labour fraught."

We enter'd on the pathway of his choice,
" *Beati Misericordes*" then he sang,
And " Now let him who conquereth rejoice."

I, with my Leader, up the mountain sprang,
Alone, and, as I went, I strove to gain
Instruction in his words, and thus began,

With eager mind : "Good Master, I would fain
Know what the spirit of Romagna meant,
Speaking of *place and consort* ?" Then again

He answer'd : " Of his soul's most evil bent
He knows the risk, thou need'st not then admire,
If he would warn, that here ye be not scant.

Because ye firmly fix your heart's desire
Where, for companionship, ye poorer seem,
Envy within your souls doth grief inspire.

If longing for the heavenly sphere supreme
Did your affections turn to things above,
Then would ye not of this as sorrow dream.

The more who in this choir celestial move,
The greater joy and gladness each doth find,

And more intensely glows with blessed love."

I said : "Now less contentment fills my mind,
Than if at first I silent had remain'd ,
And darker doubt is with my thought entwined.

How can it be that greater good is gain'd,
Where there are many to divide the spoil,
Than if its wealth by few had been retain'd ?"

Then he to me : "Because thine eyes, the while,
Are only fix'd upon the things of earth,
Amid true light thou dost in darkness toil.

The good ye find above, of highest worth,
Ineffable and Infinite, still flows
To love, as to the planet light goes forth.

The more it gives, the more with ardour glows ;
And aye, the wider charity doth reach,
To richer, fuller excellence it grows.

And still the more who gain the eternal beach,
More loveliness they find, and more they love,
And as a mirror each gives back to each.

And if my words thy doubts may not disprove,
Thou shalt see Beatrice, to give thee rest
From this and other thoughts which in thee move.

Seek only that the letters five, imprint,
As the first twain, in wounds upon thy brow,
By the sharp suff'ring quickly be erased."

I would have said : "Thou dost content me now ;"
But lo ! we had attain'd the higher zone,
And, all around, my wand'ring glance did go.

Then was I in ecstatic vision thrown,
Which me into a glorious temple bore,
Wherein were many persons ; and, alone,

There stood a woman at the gate, who wore
The sweet look of a mother.　She began :
" Why hast thou thus dealt with us ! for with sore

Distress, we sought thee sorrowing, my son."
And, as her gentle voice had ceased to speak ;
That which I look'd on faded.　Then came one,

With bitter drops of sorrow on her cheek,
The tears that are by spiteful anger worn,
Caused by the wrath which would dire vengeance
　　wreak.

She said : " If thou be ruler of the bourne
Whose name among the gods stirr'd up such strife,
And where all knowledge had its dawning morn,

Revenge thee, Pisistratus, on the life   100
Of him who dared our daughter to embrace."
Thus mildly answer'd he his haughty wife,
   With temperate look : "What may be then the
      place
For them who evil do for us desire,
If those that love us are in such ill case!"   105
   Then saw I those who, in excess of ire,
A youth were fiercely stoning ; and their cry
Was "Slay him, slay him!" Much I did admire,
   Bent downward on the earth to see him lie,
Beneath the heavy weight of coming death ;   110
Yet still his eyes were portals of the sky.
   He to his Father pray'd with his last breath
That even his murderers might pardon'd be,
And wore the aspect gentle Pity hath.
   Then, when my tranced soul again was free   115
To look on what was real, with amaze
My unfalse errors did I clearly see.
   And my good Master, who perceived me gaze
As one from whom but now his sleep hath fled,
Began : "Why walk'st with such uncertain pace ?   120

Know, that thou more than half a league hast
    sped,
With tottering limbs, and with half-closed eyes,
As one with wine or slumber in his head."

  "The things which in my vision did arise,
My gentle father, I will now declare,
What time I walk'd in such a devious wise;"

  I said, and he replied : "If thou didst wear
More than a hundred masks, I could not choose
But read the thoughts thou in thy heart dost bear.

  Thou saw'st this vision, that no vain excuse
Might be, to close thy heart unto the stream
Of peace, which the eternal founts diffuse.

  I would not of my question thou shouldst deem,
As seeing with the eyes whose light is o'er,
The while the body lies in its long dream.

  I ask'd, that thou mightst to thy steps restore
Their strength : 'tis well to hasten those who are
New-waked, to use their vigilance once more"

  We journey'd onward, 'neath the vesper-star,
More than the limit of our mortal eye
Might reach, amid the evening rays afar;

And lo! still creeping tow'rd us, there drew nigh
A cloud of densest smoke, as night obscure,
Nor from its darkness was there room to fly:

  Then unto us was lost fresh air and daylight pure 142

CANTO XVI.

Argument

Third circle, the wrathful —Discourse with Marco Lombardo
on the influence of the stars.

THE darkest cave within the place of doom,
In the blank dimness of its starless night,
Howe'er surcharged with clouds of deepest gloom,

    Shed never such a veil before my sight,
As the foul smoke which o'er that bourne did lie,
Most harsh and biting to the sense ; nor might

    The pilgrim journey with unclosed eye :
Wherefore my faithful escort to my side
Drew near, that I his strong support might try.

    Even as the blind man goes behind his guide,
That from the rightful path he may not stray,
Nor rush where pain or peril doth betide,

So through the filthy air I took my way ;
And still gave heed unto my Master's speech,
Who "See thou dost not leave me" did but say

Then I heard voices in the gloom, and each,
That all their sins be wash'd away in peace,
The Lamb of God for mercy did beseech.

Thus *Agnus Dei* they sang, and did not cease :
One word resounded through the dismal air,
In one full unison.   I said : " Are these

The sounds of spirit-voices that I hear,
My Master ?"   And he thus to me replied :
" Yea ; and of wrath the punishment they bear."

" Now who art thou who dost the smoke divide,
And speak'st as though thou wert of those who still
Count time by Calends ?"   Thus, anear my side

Was spoken.   Then my Master said : " Fulfil
The thing of which he asks thee ; and demand
If by this path we may ascend the hill."

And I : " O thou, who for the Blessed Land
Dost cleanse thee here from every earthly stain,
Thou shalt hear wonders if with me thou'lt wend."

He answer'd : " Far as may be, I would fain

Go with thee; though the smoke wherein we dwell
Hinder our sight, yet hearing doth remain."

   Then I began: "The garb, which at the knell
Of death shall pass away, still wraps me round,
And I came hither through the gates of hell.

   Since God in His great mercy me hath bound,
And would in such a wise His courts display
As, since the days of yore, no man hath found,

   Then hide not who thou wert ere death, and say
If by this path I may attain my aim.
Thus shalt thy answer guide us on our way"

   "I was a Lombard; Marco was my name;
Deep-versed in worldly wisdom, and the love
Of virtue, which hath now so poor a fame.

   To climb the hill thy footsteps rightly move."
Thus he replied; and added: "I implore
Thy prayers for me in Paradise above."

   And I to him: "I swear that on its shore
I will fulfil thy wishes; yet a doubt
From my full heart in speech must needs run o'er

   First, it was single; then again burst out
Redoubled by thy words, that show the truth,

Here and elsewhere, of this which now my thought

   Compares with thy discourse. The world, in

      sooth,

Is, as thou say'st, a waste where dwells no worth,

And fill'd and clothed with malice without ruth.

   I pray, thou wouldst the cause thereof show

      forth,

That I may see it and recount it plain ;

For one, in heaven, another on the earth

   Doth place it." Then he sigh'd a sigh of pain,

And to my question thus did he reply :

" The world is blind, my brother ; in its train

   Thou followest , and wouldst to Heaven on high

Ascribe the causes of each earthly thing,

As though controll'd by fixed necessity.

   If it were so, within your heart the spring

Of free-will were destroy'd ; nor were it right

That good should joy, and evil, sorrow bring.

   The planets rule each impulse with their might ,

But yet not all : and were it so, indeed,

To choose 'twixt good and evil ye have light,

   And free volition ; which, although it bleed,

In the first battles with the starry sphere,
Yet wins, if undismay'd, a glorious meed.

Unto a higher nature bear ye here
Allegiance ; He within you doth create
The mind which need no star malignant fear.

Thus, if the world now lies in sad estate,
In your own hearts the reason must be sought ;
As now to thee I truly will narrate.

The soul comes forth, unskill'd, unknowing aught,
From Him who look'd on it in love, before
He call'd it forth to being, out of nought.

Most like a child at play upon the shore,
Weeping and laughing at each idle toy,
Simple and ignorant of any lore ;

Save that, descended from the fount of joy,
In all things he is fain to find delight.
Deceived, he runs to that which would destroy,

If by no bridle he be train'd aright ;
And thus the law must curb him, that he still
The tower of the true city keep in sight.

Sooth, there are laws : but who doth them fulfil ?
No one , your chief the hoof doth not divide,

Though verily he ruminates at will.

And thus the people, who perceive their guide
Aim at the self-same goods for which they long,
Feed upon those, and seek not aught beside.

Well mayst thou see that, because guided wrong,
The earth is thus unto all evil hurl'd ;
Not from the sins which to your race belong.

In Rome, where erst the flag of truth unfurl'd,
There were two Suns ; that, in the days of old,
Shone on the paths of God and of the world.

Now, one to quench the other hath been bold ;
And the same hand the sword and crozier wears ·
Thus, needs, it ill hath fared within the fold.

The twain, combined, have each of each no feare .
If thou believ'st not, mark the blossom well ;
For every tree is known by what it bears.

Once truth and courtesy were wont to dwell
There where the Po and Adige do flow,
Ere Frederbck into strife and discord fell.

Now, there securely every wight may go,
Who, since some cause of shame on him hath
    come,

The face of righteous men no more may know.

　'Tis true, that in three ancient men are some
Remains of the old virtue ; and to them
The time seems long till God shall call them home :

　Gherard the Good ; Conrad Palazzo , him,
Best call'd, in French, true Lombard ; but whom ye,
Besides, do Guido da Castello name.

　I tell thee, that the Church of Rome thou'lt see
(Because it joins two diverse rules in one)
Dragg'd through the mud, and both all filthy be."

　" Well hast thou said, O Marco," I began ;
" And now I plainly see the cause for which
The sons of Levi heritage had none.

　But who is that Gherardo whom thy speech
Proclaims a remnant of the glorious dead,
Whose virtue to this wicked age still preach ?"

　He said : " Thy words have proved me or misled,
If thou the good Gherardo dost not know ;
And yet in Tuscan tongue thy words are said.

　For by no other surname doth he go,
If from his daughter Gaia be not drawn
Some appellation.　Now farewell, for lo !

Through the thick smoke is whitening the dawn,

In silver light : I must depart, before

There comes the guardian angel of the zone "

    He turn'd away, and to my words gave ear no

       more.

CANTO XVII.

Argument.

Dante and Virgil come forth from the thick smoke, the symbol
of anger.—In a vision, Dante sees three examples of this
passion.—He is conducted by an Angel to the fourth
circle, where sloth is punished.—Virgil discourses concerning envy.

Hast thou e'er seen how, on some Alpine height,

Enfolded in thick mist, thou didst perceive

No more than doth a mole, the sunny light?

And when the vapours moist and dense, that weave

A veil around thee, 'gin to melt away,

Weakly the pallid sunbeams they receive.

This image feebly may to thee convey

The manner in which now I saw at last

The orb that near its couch of slumber lay.

Still slowly in my Master's steps I pass'd

Forth from the dimness to the light, which now
Only on the far summits had its root.

  O Fancy, by whose power full oft we go
Wrapp'd in our thoughts from every outward thing,
Unheeding, did a thousand trumpets blow,

  Whence is thy hidden and unsensual spring ?
I ween, thou art impell'd by purer light,
Or self-existent or which Heaven doth bring.

  Now was reveal'd unto my inward sight,
She who, for guilt, was doom'd the form to wear
Of the sweet bird whose song doth most delight

  And thus my thoughts were so restricted here
In their own depths, that to my mental eye
Nought from without might enter nor appear.

  Then in my trance I saw, uplifted high,
A gallows; and thereon, in scornful mood,
Hung one who did without repentance die.

  Around, the great Ahasuerus stood,
Esther his wife, and righteous Mordecai,
Who in both deeds and words alike was good.

  And as the pictured fancy pass'd away,
Even like a bubble bursting, when doth fail

The wat'ry film beneath which erst it lay,
    Before me a fair maiden seem'd to wail,
With many tears   And thus who spake : "O queen,
Why in thy wrath didst thou thyself assail,
    From fear to lose Lavinia ?   Now, I ween,
For ever thou hast lost me ; more I sigh,
My mother, for the grief which thee hath slain,

    Than for aught else"   As, when in sleep we lie,
The closed lids are lit by sudden gleam,
And slumber trembles ere it wholly die,
    Thus fled the imagery of my dream,
Soon as the radiance on my forehead lay,
More bright than ye on this dark earth may deem.

    I turn'd to see whence came the dazzling ray,
And heard a voice which said · "Now here ascend ,"
And then all other thoughts I put away,
    And did my heart and will so wholly bend,
That I for him who spoke to me might seek,
I rested not till I this knowledge gain'd.

    As, when upon our sight the sunbeams break,
So bright, their splendours o'er our senses prevail ;
Even thus, to bear that vision I was weak.

" Behold a heavenly One, who will not fail,
Unask'd, to guide our steps unto the skies ;
Around him his own glory weaves a veil.

He acts toward us in the self-same wise
As we do with ourselves ; he doth despite
Unto the prayer, who waits till it arise.

Obey we now the voice that doth invite ;
Strive to ascend ere comes the twilight dim ;
For, alas, we may not till the dawning light

Return." Thus spake my guide ; and I with him
To the steep pathway strove my steps to bring.
And when I to the earliest grade had come,

Methought the floating of an angel's wing
A moment fann'd my forehead, as he sped,
And " Blessed are the peaceful" seem'd to sing ;

And now above our heads the light is fled
Of the last sunbeam fading into night,
And o'er the heavens the starry hosts are led.

" Why feel I such diminish'd strength and might ?"
I said within myself ; because all power
I lost, it seem'd, to guide my footsteps right.

We now had come to where the stair no more

Ascends ; and firmly fix'd we did appear,
Even as a ship when it hath touch'd the shore.

   I listen'd, all intent, that I might hear
Some word or sound, this new abode within ;
And then I turn'd me to my Master dear,

   And spake : " My gentle father, say, what sin
Is cleansed here !   Although our feet be stay'd,
Stay not thy words."   Then thus did he begin :

   " The love of virtue, which by sloth was made
Too weak to reach its aim, ye here renew ;
And here ye ply the oar too long delay'd.

   But that more clearly this may greet thy view,
Turn thou thy thoughts to me ; and thou shalt find
Of this our sojourn some good fruit ensue.

   Ne'er was Creator or created mind,"
Thus he went on, " my son, without some love,
Thou know'st, by Nature or the soul assign'd.

   And never Nature may to error move ;
But if the soul on evil object light,
Or if too small or great the force it prove,

   Then doth it wander from the path of right.
First, love the best ; then, be in measure worn

The second: and thou'lt seek no ill delight.

But if thou stray to evil, or dost burn
Too much, or with too little zeal for good,
Against the Maker his own works ye turn.

Hence, it may well by thee be understood,
Love is the seed of virtue and each deed
That ye bewail beyond the evil flood.

And, because love must evermore give heed
To its belovèd's welfare, it must be
That from their proper hate all things are freed.

Since no created being can ye see,
Or self-existent, or from God apart,
The finite may not hate Infinity.

Thus it remains, if well I know this art,
Your neighbour's hurt ye love ; and, in three ways,
This love is born within your earthly heart.

There are who hope that they themselves may raise,
Upon their neighbour's downfall ; and they claim
For this, that he be sunk to lower place.

There are who glory, honour, power, and fame
Would fear to lose, if others upward rise ;
And thus, in heart, they love their neighbour's blame.

There are who, injured, would in wrathful guise
Desire to gloat o'er the avenging blow,
And thus their neighbour's hurt do they devise.

Thus threefold love, within the scene below,
Is wept ; I would the other thou shouldst learn,
Which unto good doth in ill measure go.

Each one confus'dly tow'rd some good doth turn,
On which his spirit rests with strong desire ;
And to attain it every heart doth burn.

Those who too slowly, upon earth, acquire
The love of virtue (if but they repent)
Purged in this circle, heavenward may aspire.

And there are joys which cannot give content ;
True happiness they are not, nor the root
And essence of the true and excellent.

The love which too much feeds on earthly fruit,
Above us is 'n triple scene they mourn :
But of its threefold parting am I mute,

For thou thyself must go to seek it in that bourne.

CANTO XVIII.

Argument.

Virgil continues his discourse, and defends the doctrine of freewill.—Dante is roused from his meditations by different voices, exhorting to diligence; after which he falls into a deep sleep.

My lofty teacher now had ceased to speak,
And look'd at me intently, to perceive
If I of him would further knowledge seek.

And as his words a greater thirst did leave,
Silent without, within myself I said:
"Perchance my too much asking doth him grieve"

But this true father who my footsteps led,
And saw the timid wish within my mind,
Speaking, of speech much boldness in me bred,

Whence I: "My Master, in thy light I find
Mine eyes so strengthen'd that I clearly see
The things which by thy words are said or sign'd.

Therefore I pray, sweet father, that to me
Thou wouldst explain this love, from whence it seems
All good works come, and those which evil be."

"Direct," he said, "toward me the bright beams
Of thought; while unto thee the fault I prove
Of him, who, blind, himself a leader dooms.

The soul which is created apt for love,
Soon as by joy awaken'd to discern,
Toward each pleasant thing doth quickly move;

And, rous'd within you, Fantasy doth learn
The pictured forms of all things to unfold,
So that unto themselves your hearts they turn.

And if, when moved to that which ye behold,
Your soul inclines toward it, such desire
Is love, which Nature doth within you hold.

Thus, as the flame still ever mounteth higher,
Because, as in its form is well exprest,
It must ascend unto the fount of fire;

Even so the soul by strong desire imprest,
(Which is a spiritual motion,) till it find
The thing which is belov'd, can take no rest.

Now mayst thou see, in sooth, how they are blind,

Who still aver that every loving heart
May be as good and laudable defined.

Perchance, the stuff whereof their love is blent
Is always good , but yet not every seal
Is good, although the wax be excellent."

"Thy words to my attentive thought reveal,"
I said, "the nature with which love is fraught ;
But now thereby a greater doubt I feel.

For, if affection from without be brought,
And with no other foot the soul may move,
In good or ill of merit there is nought."

And he to me : " What reason may, I prove ;
That which belongs to faith thou then shalt learn
When Beatrice descendeth from above.

Each form substantial (as thou mayst discern)
Distinct from matter, and therewith combined,
Hath special strength, that in itself is worn .

Which strength, except it work, ye cannot find,
Nor feel, nor show, unless by the effoot ;
As life is by a plant's green foliage sign'd

Yet none can tell whence comes the intellect,
The dawn of earliest knowledge which ye see

And the first instincts that your hearts affect,
　　Dwelling in you, as in the honey-bee
Her studious labour ; and this first intent
Alike from praise or blame is ever free.
　　Now, though to this all other thoughts were bent,
Innate in you is virtue which controls,
And ought to hold the bridle of assent.
　　This is the principle on which your souls
Meet for reward or punishment are found,
As your desire on good or evil falls.
　　Those who have search'd into the deep profound
Perceived this innate liberty of will ;
Thus in the world their moral maxims sound.
　　But say that, of necessity, do fill
Your hearts the strong desires which in you flame ,
Yet power is given you to restrain them still.
　　And noble virtue Beatrice doth name
Volition ; see thou think'st thereon aright,
What time with her thou speak'st."　The moon-light came
　　　　．
　　More tardy, tow'rd the mid-hour of the night,
Most like a goblet that is all a-glow ;

And made the stars shine forth with rarer light.

And 'gainst the sky did by that pathway go,
Lit by the sun, when those of Rome behold,
'Twixt Sards and Corsicans, it lying low.

And he by whom Pietola doth hold
A nobler name than e'er the Mantuan town,
From me my heavy burden had unroll'd.

For now the clearest light of reason shone
Upon the doubts which did my heart dismay,
And I remain'd as one on whom is thrown

A dreamy chain of slumber. But away .
At once my sleep was chased by a vast crowd
Who follow'd us. As olden legends say,

Asopus and Ismenus heard the loud
And furious multitude rush past by night,
To celebrate the rites to Bacchus vow'd;

So those who now came forward in our sight
Were running with the eager steps of haste,
By righteous love and will impell'd aright.

Full soon our slower speed they overpast,
And swiftly that great multitude swept by;
And two cried out with tears, still hurrying fast.

" With haste did Mary to the mountain fly ;
And the great Cæsar first Marseilles subdues,
Then quickly Lerida in Spain doth try."

" Now speed we, speed, that we no time may lose
For lack of love," the others then replied :
" Good study the green leaves of grace renews "

" O ye in whom such fervour doth abide,
Whereby, perchance, your negligent delay
And lukewarmness in good is now supplied,

This man, who lives, (and I no falsehood say),
Would fain ascend when the first sunbeams break ;
Then tell us where to find the upward way ; "

These words to them did gentle Virgil speak.
" Now follow in our steps," the Shades replied ,
" And ye shall find the entrance which ye seek.

Within us such deep longing doth abide,
We may not stay , then pardon, if perchance
Our zeal seem to discourtesy allied.

I was the Abbot of St. Zeno once,
In fair Verona, 'neath the sway of him
Who hath made Milan weep her sore mischance,

The excellent Barbarossa.   To the dim

And 'gainst sepulchre descendeth one

Who soon shall mourn that e'er his hand hath
   come

  Upon our convent, for his base-born son,

Deform'd in body, more deform'd in mind,

In the true pastor's place." As he went on,

  I know not if more words were on the wind

Dispersed, so far already had he sped :

But these within my memory did I bind,

  And he who ever came unto mine aid,

Thus spake · " Now turn thee hither and behold

Two who do here reprove for sloth." Then said

  They, behind all the rest · " In days of old,

Those who pass'd through the waters died, before

Their heirs might see the land where Jordan roll'd.

  And those who, weary of the toil they bore,

Slothful did from Anchises' son depart,

A life without or praise or glory wore "

  Now when they were from us so far apart

That they had wholly vanish'd from our sight,

New questionings arose within my heart,

  New thoughts whereon my fancy did alight ;

The which of such strange sweetness did I deem,
I closed my eyelids in a vague delight,
   And all my thinking pass'd into a dream.

CANTO XIX.

Argument

Vision of the Poet, and ascent to the Fifth Circle, where
Avarice is punished.—Pope Adrian V.

Now when the heat of day no more hath power
To lend its warmth unto the moon's chill beam,
Conquer'd by Earth or Saturn, in the hour
  When magno sees its greatest fortune gleam,
Before the dawn, in the far orient sky,
Arising in the twilight's silver stream,
  I saw a woman hideous and awry,
The while I slept; who seem'd of stammering speech,
Maim'd in her hands, and with distorted eye,
  And hvid hue. But as the sunbeams reach
The limbs all chill'd beneath the damps of night,
Even so my gaze to her appear'd to teach

Sweet language, and her features smooth'd aright,
Till her foul form and vision's twisted ray
Shone in the beauty of love's rosy light.

And when her tongue was loos'd, she sang a lay
So lovely that thereto my heart was bound,
Nor from her music might I turn away.

She sang: "I am the syren of sweet sound,
Charming the mariners amid the sea,
For in my voice such melody is found.

I drew Ulysses from his path to me,
With my sweet singing: they who with me dwell
Rarely depart; therein such joys there be."

Scarce had she closed her song of magic spell,
When one appear'd, in holy light array'd,
To bring dismay to her so false and fell.

"O Virgil, Virgil, who is this?" she said,
And in her mien a righteous anger wore;
While on her radiant form his eyes were stay'd.

She took the foul one, and her garments tore,
And show'd to me the loathsome form within;
I woke with the ill savour that it bore.

I oped my eyes; thus Virgil did begin:

" Thrice have I said to thee, ' Arise and go ; '
Seek we the spot where we may entrance win."

I rose ; the morning sunbeams shed a glow
On all the circles of the sacred hill,
And their bright radiance fell behind us now.

Walking as one whom pensive musings fill
With thoughts that cause him tow'rd the earth to bend,
I went, in form of arch half curved still ;

And heard : " Now come, for here ye may ascend,"
Said in a voice so sweet and so benign,
As never spake in this our mortal land.

With swanlike wings, a lovely form divine
Disclosed whereby we might attain the height,
'Twixt the two walls which did the path confine ;

Then touch'd us with his plumes of snowy white :
Affirming that the mourning hearts are blest,
For they at last shall be consoled aright.

" Wherefore upon the earth thy glances rest
In such a wise ?" to me began my guide,
When from the angel we had somewhat pass'd.

" Such doubt is raised within me," I replied,
" By a new vision, whose strange memories cleave

So close I cannot part them from my side."

"Saw'st thou the ancient witch, by whom they grieve
Solely above us in each painful song?"
He said, "and how her nets ye still may leave?

It is enough; with greater haste speed on:
Turn thou thine eyes unto the starry sky,
The heavenly lure that circles round the throne

Of the Eternal Sire.   As, ere it fly,
The falcon first looks downwards at its feet,
Then spreads its wings unto its master's cry,

Even so did I; and where the wall was split
In twain, we, climbing, toil'd, until once more
A level surface did our footsteps greet.

And as this fifth abode we journey'd o'er,
Some spirits there I saw, who seem'd to grieve,
Low lying on the earth with wailings sore.

They said: "My soul unto the dust doth cleave,"
And mournfully they spake with groans and sighs
So deep, their words I hardly might perceive.

"O ye Elect of God, on whom there lies
A woe by hope and justice made more light,
Aid us to find where we may heavenward rise."

" If ye, who now advance with form upright,
Would find the upward path most speedily,
Let your left hand be still toward the height."

Thus ask'd the Poet, and thus answer'd he
Who grovell'd near our steps.   Even so I learn'd
The thing which with mine eyes I might not see :

And unto Virgil then my glance I turn'd :
Wherefore with gesture kind he gave assent
To that for which my eager-spirit yearn'd.

And when my longing I might thus content,
To him who now had spoken I drew near,
Because his words had fix'd my thoughts intent.

I said : " O thou whose weeping doth repair
The sin with which thou canst not turn to God,
Defer awhile for me thy greater care.

Say who thou wert, and wherefore on the sod
Thou liest prone , and if thou wouldst that they
Who still have life should aid thee on thy road."

And he to me : " Why God on us doth lay
This grief, I will declare to thee ; but learn,
I was on earth the heir of Peter's sway.

Between Chiaveri and Sestri's hourne

Flows a fair stream, and from its name is known
The title by my ancient lineage worn.

A month, and little more, on me was thrown
The mantle which to him who keeps it clean
Weighs so that all besides seems light as down.

And late, alas! my penitence hath been;
But life her false delusion did disclose,
When I of Rome was pastor   Then, I ween,

Saw I that there I might not find repose;
Yet none on earth was higher: thus my heart
Unto the love of heavenly life arose.

Till then, my soul was sad, and kept apart
From God, by avil greediness of gain,
Now, as thou seest, I suffer here the smart.

The ill by avarice done is shown most plain,
In that endured by those within this bound;
Nor hath the mountain a more bitter pain.

Even as in life our eyes were ever found
Intent on earthly things, nor look'd on high,
Thus justice here hath fix'd them on the ground.

As greed of gain caused purer love to die,
Whence all our works were fruitless and in vain,

Thus justice forces us on earth to be,

    While binding cords our hands and feet detain ,

As long as it our Heavenly Sire shall please,

So long we must immovable remain."

    I would have answer'd, kneeling on my knees ;

But as I now began, and he perceived

My humble attitude, as one who sees

    Only by listening, nor is deceived,

He said : "Why bend thee unto earth so low ?"

And I : " Because in conscience I were grieved,

    If to thy rank I did no reverence show."

He answer'd : " Rise, my brother, thou hast err'd ,

For I am but God's servant, even as thou.

    If o'er the holy evangelic word

That neque nubent says, were understood

By thee, thou hadst perceived what I infer'd.

    But now depart : no longer time I would

Thou shouldst remain ; because, in sooth, thy stay

Hinders my sorrow's purifying flood.

    I have a niece, Alagia, who aye

Was of a gentle spirit ; if our ill

Example have not guided her astray :

    She, of my race, alone on earth remaineth still."

CANTO XX.

———

ILL fights the will when one more strong hath will'd,
Against my pleasure, for my guide's content,
I drew the pitcher from the stream unfill'd.

Along the rock I with my leader went,
There where the pathway for our steps was clear,
As one who clings unto a battlement;

For those who from their eyes in many a tear
Shed forth the sin throughout the world dispers'd,
Toward the precipice were placed too near.

O ancient wolf, be thou for aye accurs'd,
Who more than any other seek'st thy prey,
Because of thy dark greed and ravening thirst!

Ye skies, within whose sphere, as some do say,
There dwells a power o'er all things here below,
When cometh he who shall this creature slay?

Onward we went, with paces soft and slow,
And still my mind was fix'd upon each Shade
Who wept around me with the voice of woe.

And now by chance I heard, "Sweet Mary," said,
Before us, with complainings sad and wild,
As one who in her sorrow travailèd;

And then : "Thou wert a maiden poor and mild,
As by the lowly birthplace we may know,
Where meekly thou didst lay thy holy child."

And afterwards I heard : "Fabricius, thou   .
Didst rather poverty with virtue seek,
Than riches whereunto foul crime did grow."

In these his words I did such pleasure take,
That I with eager footsteps quickly sped
To look on him who in such accents spake.

Now he recounted the great largess shed
By Nicholas upon the maidens three,
That their young life in honour might be led.

"O thou whose words so fair and righteous be,"

Thus I began, "say who thou wert, and why
Those worthy praises still are sung by thee

Not without thanks shall be thy speech, if I
Return to fill the measure upon earth
Of the short life that to its goal doth fly."

And he : " It shall be told ; yet not for worth
Which thence I look for : but because in thee,
While yet in life, such heavenly grace shines forth.

I was the root of the most evil tree,
Whose deathly shade all Christendom doth fill,
So that from thence no wholesome fruit may be

If there were power in Douay, Bruges, Lille,
Or Ghent, full soon revenge ye should behold ;
Which to the Heavenly Judge I pray for still.

When erst on earth, Hugh Capet was I call'd ,
From me each Philip and each Louis won
The right that o'er the realm of France they hold

I of a Paris butcher was the son ;
For when the ancient kings had pass'd away,
Save one in dusky raiment all alone,

Firmly within my hands the bridle lay,
Which govern'd the whole kingdom , and such power

For what I then acquired, and full array

  Of friends, that I uplifted in that hour

My son to wear the widow'd diadem ·

Thence sprang the royal line.   But till the dower

  Of fair Provence destroy'd all modest shame,

Remaining still mid my fierce lawless band,

Its worth was small, yet thence small evil came.

  Now it began with lies and with high hand

Its rapine, then it seized, to make amends,

Ponthieu and Gascony and Normanland.

  And next, in Italy, to make amends,

Charles slew Conradin, to heavenly life,

St. Thomas then he sent, to make amends.

  Not long had pass'd ere, in a time of strife,

I saw another Charles come forth from France,

To show the craft with which his race is rife

  He came unarm'd, and only with the lance

Of Judas, but so sharp the point it bore,

Unto the heart of Florence did it glance.

  From thence, not land but sin and hatred sore

He shall obtain; and that so much more grave,

As it to him a lighter aspect wore.

The other newly captured on the wave
I now behold ; he doth his daughter sell,
Even as a Corsair bargains for a slave.

O Avarice, thou canst not be more fell,
Since thou unto thyself my race canst turn
And thence all care of their own flesh expel !

That past and future ill we less may scorn,
Within Alagna comes the flour-de-lis,
And in his vicar Christ is captive borne.

And Him derided once again I see ;
Again renew'd the vinegar and gall,
And 'twixt new thieves He hangeth on the tree.

Another Pilate in the judgment-hall
I see ; so cruel, that unsated still
His lawless hands upon the temple fall.

O God ! when comes the morning that shall fill
My heart with gladness, and the vengeance rouse
That sweetens wrath within thy secret will !

Know, what I spake of her, the Blessed Spouse
Of the most Holy Spirit, and which led
Thee tow'rds me, longing that I should disclose

Still more, continually by us is said,

While yet the daylight with us doth abide ;
At dusk, we tell a sadder tale instead.

　　We sung the story of Pygmalion's pride,
Who work'd his lawless will from love of gold ,
A thief, a traitor, and a parricide.   105

　　The wretchedness of Midas we unfold,
That erst fulfill'd his avaricious prayer ;
Even now ye laugh, whene'er the tale is told.

　　And we remember Achan's folly here,
Who stole the spoils ; he in our speech renews   110
The pain which Joshua's anger made him bear.

　　Sapphira with her husband we accuse ;
We praise the scourge which Heliodorus chased .
And round the mount in infamy diffuse

　　His name who Polydorus slew.　And last   115
We all cry out ᛫ 'O Crassus, tell us now
(For well thou knowest it) how gold doth taste.'

　　And sometimes speak we loud and sometimes low ,
Even as the grief which on our souls doth weigh
More swift or slower from our lips may flow.   120

　　In the good words which we discourse by day,
I was not all alone ; but where thou wert

None other raised his voice."   Upon our way,

Already from those Shades we did depart,
Still striving to o'ercome the arduous path,
With the great eagerness that fill'd my heart.

Now, as if shaken by the stormwind's breath,
The mountain trembled, and I shudder'd, even
As one who is led forth unto his death.

Less wildly, sure, of old was Delos driven,
Before Latona there a refuge made,
To bring forth the twin starry eyes of heaven.

Then such a cry arose, that he who led
My steps came near, and said : " Be of good cheer,
I ever guide thee : be not thou afraid."

And " *Gloria in excelsis* " did I hear ;
All voices join'd the strain, with ready will,
Far as the music came unto mine ear.

Silent we stood, as once on Bethlehem's hill
The shepherds who first heard that angel-song,
Until the trembling ceased and they were still.

And now we pass'd our holy path along,
Gazing the while upon the Shades who wept
Lowly on earth, in sooth, a mournful throng.

No ignorance in me hath ever kept
Such longing thirst for knowledge, as, I ween,
(If my remembrance have not err'd or slept,)
    Within my anxious mind I suffer'd then;
But, in our haste, I might no answer seek,
Nor yet anear me might there aught be seen:
    Thus went I on my way, in pensive thought
        meek.

CANTO XXI.

—•—

Now woke within my mind the longing thirst,
Unslaked, save where Samaria's daughter sought
The fountain from which living waters burst.

Behind my guide, with eager musings fraught,
In haste along the cumber'd way I sped,
Mourning for this just penalty, in thought.

And lo! as, in the Gospel, Luke hath said
That by the two disciples Christ was seen,
Loosed from the sepulchre where he was laid,

Even thus a Shade appear'd to us, I ween,
Upon the grovelling crowd he gazed adown,
And then he spake to us with gentle mien.

•

" My brothers, may God's peace by you be known."
Quickly we turn'd, to hear that voice's sound,
And Virgil greeted him and thus began :

" By thee may overlasting peace be found,
And the redoom'd, anear the throne of Him
Who in eternal exile me hath bound."

He answered : " Why and wherefore would ye climb
This mount, if God doth hold you in disdain !
And who hath led you through the pathway dim ! "

And Virgil thus : " Behold the signs of pain,
On this man's brow ; writ by the sword of light,
As proof that with the blessèd he shall reign,

At least   Since she who toileth day and night,
Not yet for him hath meted out the line,
Which Clotho spins for every living wight,

His soul, which is akin to thine and mine,
Might not attempt alone the upward way,
Because he sees not with immortal eyne.

Thus was I summon'd to the light of day,
From the deep mouth of Hades ; to instruct
His steps, as far as knowledge in me lay.

But tell us why but now the mountain rock'd,

And wherefore all cried out, as with one voice,
From hence to where the land is ocean-look'd."

Now at this question much did I rejoice ;
I thought : " It may be that I here shall slake
The thirst which thus my longing soul annoys."

Then he began   " Here no event may break
The order'd rule of measured sanctity,
Nor for itself a lawless course can make.

From chance and change we here are wholly free,
But when a soul is ready for the sky,
The trembling of the mountain needs must be.

For never rain, nor hail, nor snow, may lie
Upon this hill ; nor dew, nor frosty air,   •
Than the short staircase may ascend more high.

No cloud doth ever rise nor oft nor rare,
Nor lightning flash, nor Thaumas' daughter sweet,
Whose form appears on earth, now here, now there.

No higher may the stormy vapours fleet,
Than to the steps of which but now I spake,
Whereon St. Peter's Vicar rests his feet.

Beneath, the mountain more or less may shake :
But here for prison'd winds, I know not how,

The shuddering earthquake never doth awake.

Only the trembling of the hill we know,
Whene'er some spirit, purified, would rise ;
Then chaunts of praise are sung by high and low

In will alone the proof of cleanness lies ,
Which Will, that may to heavenly realms aspire,
With its new power the spirit doth surprise.

And it had earlier soar'd , but the desire
Implanted by God's justice, here is bent,
As erst on sin, now on the penal fire.

And I who to this punishment was sent,
Till full five hundred years their course should roll,
But now have known free will for the ascent.

Thus thou hast felt the earthquake ; and each soul,
On all the mountain, renders holy praise :
For which I would they soon may reach their goal "

He spake : as when the cooling stream allays
Tormenting thirst, I have no power to tell
What joy within my heart his words did raise.

Then my wise Leader said : " Now see I well
The net that holds you, and the way to flee ;
And why the mountain trembles where ye dwell,

And ye rejoice.   I pray thee, tell to me
Thy name, and wherefore centuries have roll'd,
While this hath been a prison house for thee ?"

"When the good Titus, in the days of old,
By aid from God took vengeance of the wounds
Whence issued forth the blood by Judas sold,"

The Shade replied, "the name that most resounds
And longest, wore I when in life , but faith
I had not yet, though to earth's furthest bounds

My fame went forth.   So sweet my vocal breath,
I, of Toulouse, my lays to Rome did bring ;
And there my forehead wore the myrtle wreath.

Statius my earthly name ; erst did I sing
Of Thebes, then of Achilles great in fight ;
But sank ere I my second goal might win.

My ardour sprang from out the sparks of light,
The burning radiance of the flame divine,
From whence a thousand minds have learn'd aright ;

The Æneid I would say ; dear mother mine ;
And gentle nurse of each poetic strain :
Else had I never writ one worthy line.

Might I to look on Virgil once attain,

Another year full gladly had I borne,
More than is due, within this place of pain."

   Then, at these words, to me did Virgil turn, .
Commanding silence with a silent glance;
But not at will may strength be ever worn:

   For smiles and tears so quickly oft advance,
Behind the thoughts from whence they each arose,
That will more slowly moves. Thus did it chance,

   I smiled as one in whom some secret lies,
And then the spirit stay'd his speech, the while
He gazed to read the meaning in my eyes.

   " As thou wouldst win the guerdon of thy toil,"
He said, " now tell me wherefore on thy brow
There shone the sudden lightening of a smile."

   On either side was I perplexed now :
One bade me hush, the other fain would make
Me speak. And the debate my looks did show

   Was understood. " Fear not," thus Virgil spake,
" To tell the truth; for now mayst thou declare
The thing which he so eagerly doth seek."

   Then I began . " Thou in thy thought dost bear
Much wonder at the smile which thou hast seen;

But for a greater marvel now prepare,

  O ancient Shade. This man, on whom I lean,

Is that same Virgil who hath taught so well   125

To sing of Gods and men. If there have been

  In thee some doubt, let it no longer dwell

Within thy mind, but now receive as true

The words which unto thee of him I tell."

  Then to embrace my Leader's knees he drew   130

Anear; but Virgil said: " My brother, stay;

For thou, a Shade, dost here a Shade pursue."

  He rose and spake: " Now mayst thou justly weigh

The love for thee wherewith my heart is rife;

When thoughts of our vain semblance pass'd away,   135

  And I of shadows doem'd as having mortal life."

CANTO XXII.

The angel-guide was left behind us now,

Who to the sixth abode our steps had led,

While he erased a letter from my brow,

  And, "They whose hearts on righteousness are

    stay'd,"

He sung, "are crown'd with joy , and ever blest

Are those who thirst :" no more the words he said.

  More lightly than at first I onward press'd ,

For without labour I might there aspire,

And swift as airy spirits now I pass'd.

  When Virgil thus began : " The love whose fire

Is lit by virtue, if its outward flame

Appear, responsive ardour doth inspire.

Therefore since Juvenal among us came
Unto the land of Hades, and to me
Reveal'd the love thou hadst unto my name,

Such loving kindness bore I unto thee,
As never yet was felt for one unknown ;
Thus, brief this steep ascent now seems to be.

But say, and pardon me if I have shown
Too daring freedom in the question bold,
And speak with me as with a friend alone,

How could thy breast so much of avarice hold,
Amid the studious lore thou didst approve,
And which to thee did highest truths unfold ?"

My Master's words the spirit seem'd to move
Unto a shadowy smile ; and then he said :
" Thy every speech to me is sign of love.

Full often does the truth appear, array'd
In such a wise that it may well deceive,
For the true reasons which therein are stay'd.

Thy question shows me that thou dost believe
The love of hoarding was my earthly vice,
Perchance from the abode which now we leave.

But know, that from my heart was avarice
Too far apart ; thus have I felt the pain,
For many thousand moons, of that excess.

And had I not endeavour'd to attain
To virtue, when I heard thy voice, which call'd,
(Wrathful against our human nature's stain,)

'Why dost not rule, accursèd love of gold,
The appetite of man for earthly things?'
In the sad tournament my fate were told.

Then I perceived that all too wide the wings
Of largess might be spread ; and thus my eyes
Shed tears for this and other sin it brings.

And many a soul at the last day shall rise
With close cut locks, because he hath not known
That man must aye repent him ere he dies.

The fault that from another sin hath gone
To the extreme of difference, here, I ween,
Join'd with its opposite must make its moan.

And therefore I among the band have been,
Who here bewail their avaricious ways,
Because the contrary in me was seen."

" But when thou erst didst sing the rude affrays

Of them, Jocasta's double cause of woe,"
Thus spake the Singer of the pastoral lays,

"By that which Clio there with thee doth show,
It seems thou didst not yet possess aright
The faith without which heaven we may not know.

If it be thus, what sun or radiant light
Flooded the darkness, when thy sails behind
The Galilean Fisher took their flight ?"

He answer'd him : " At first by thee inclined,
I drank the rills that from Parnassus flow ;
Thereafter God illumined all my mind.

Thou didst as they who in the darkness go,
Holding a light which yet they cannot use ;
But unto those behind, the way doth show.

There where thou saidst : 'The world its growth
        renews ;
Again its early spring-time it shall see,
And Heaven once more new progeny diffuse.'

By thee a poet ; Christian, too, by thee
Was I : but that thou well mayst comprehend,
Portray'd in brighter hues my speech shall be.

Already, earth was fill'd on every hand

With the true faith, dispersed by those who brought
The joyful tidings of the eternal land;
　And these thy words with the same tones were
　　fraught
As the discourse of those new preachers bore;
Therefore unto their teaching oft I sought.

　And then to me so holy seem'd their lore,
That, when Domitian chased them unto death,
For their sad sufferings I bewailèd sore.

　Even while I lived the life of earthly breath,
The thought of their pure ways made me contemn
The rites and creed of every other faith.

　And ere I led the Greeks unto the stream
Of Thebes in poesy, the holy rite
Baptismal did I seek, but yet did seem

　Long time a heathen to all outward sight:
And for this sloth I dwelt in the fourth zone,
Four times a hundred years, in doleful plight.

　Thou who hast raised the dusky curtain drawn
Before mine eyes, while yet I might ascend,
Ere time of penitence and prayer was gone,

　Say, where is Terence now, our ancient friend?

Cæcilius, Plautus, Varro!   On what shore
Have they their dwelling, in the mournful land!"

"Persius and they, and I, and many more,"   100
My Leader thus replied, " now dwell with him,
The Greek the Muses loved in days of yore,

In the first circle of the prison dim ;
And oft discourse we of the mount whence flow
The rills that nurture the poetic stream.   105

Euripides, Anacreon, with us go ;
And Agatho, and many a Grecian wise,
Who round their foreheads twined the laurel bough

There dwells Simonides, in mournful guise
And those of whom thou erst didst sing are there ;   110
Antigone, Ismene with sad eyes ;

And there ye see Tiresias' daughter fair ;
Deiphile, Argia with us dwell,
And Thetis, with the sea-flowers in her hair ;

And she who show'd where Langia's fountains well,   115
And mild her eastern, Deidamia."   Now,
Emerging from the pathway's rocky cell,

Silent the poet gazed around ; for lo !
Four of the Maidens of the Day had fled,

And by his chariot wheel the fifth did go.   120

   " Methinks it now were well," my Leader said,

" Our right hand tow'rd the mountain's verge to turn,

Circling around the hill as erst we sped."

   Thus from accustom'd use we here did learn ,

And with less doubtful mind we journey'd on,   125

For in that other Shade we might discern

   Consent.   Together did they pass ; alone

I follow'd, listening to the words which there

They spake, from whom I poesy had known.

   But soon was broken this discoursing fair ;   130

For midway in the path a tree did grow,

Whose fruit shed forth an odour sweet and rare.

   And as the fir-tree's still ascending bough

Grows less and less, so this as it descends :

I think, that none may to the summit go.   135

   And from the rampart which our path defends,

There fell a stream of water cool and clear,

And with the foliage green its soft shower blends.

   Now the two Poets to the tree drew near,

And then a voice among the leaves we heard,   140

Crying : " This fruit ye may not eat of here ;"

Then said : " The impulse which in Mary stirr'd
Was for the honour of the nuptials, more
Than to refresh the lips whose gentle word

Doth plead for you.   The Roman dames, of yore,
Drank only water : less did Daniel doom
Of food, than of acquiring heavenly lore.

The world's first ages shone with golden gleam,
When hunger made the acorn sweet and good ;
And nectar flow'd, with thirst, in every stream.

Locusts and honey were the simple food
That fed the Baptist in the desert drear :
Thus is his name with glorious praise endued,

For evermore ; as in the Gospel ye may hear."

CANTO XXIII.

Argument.

Dante finds, among the gluttonous, his friend Forese, who
praises the virtues of his wife, and reproves the vices of the
Florentine ladies.

THE while I fix'd my eyes on the green leaves,
Intently looking with the gaze of one
Who the small song-birds of their life bereaves,

My more than father said to me : "My son,
Now let us hasten on ; for it is meet   5
To profit by the day, ere it is done."

I quickly turn'd me then ; and not less fleet
My footsteps were, that I might draw anear
The wise, whose words made the long journey sweet.

In mingled wail and singing did I hear .   10
" My lips shall praise thee, Lord ;" the holy strain
Delight and sorrow to my soul did bear.

"What sound is this, issuing from the plain,"
I said, "my gentle father!"   He replied :
"Those Shades fulfil their duty mid their pain."

As when the thoughtful pilgrim hath espied
One who is all unknown, he doth not stay,
But looks toward him and then turns aside ;

Thus, following us more quickly on the way,
Joining and passing us, that band devout
Gazed upon us, but yet no word did say.

Their hollow eyes with dusky gloom were fraught :
Their cheeks were pallid , and their frames so lean,
Moulding the skin the bones might well be sought.

Less meagre Erisicthon's frame, I ween,
When, to the last extreme of hunger led,
Most fierce his famish'd sufferings had been.

I thought within myself, and thus I said :
"Behold Jerusalem's citizens, when one,
A Jewish mother, on her infant fed."

Their eyes seem'd rings from whence the gems were
        gone ;
And those who Omo on man's brow descry,
In theirs, in sooth, the M might well have known.

Who would believe that in this fruit could lie
Such strong dominion by its sweet perfume,
Or in the crystal stream, unknowing why?

I marvell'd much concerning this their doom;
Because the reason yet I did not learn
Of their sad leanness and their meagre gloom.

When lo! the sunken eyes toward me turn
Of one among those shadowy forms, who said,
With a loud voice: "What grace to me is borne?"

Remembrance of that Shade from me had fled;
But yet his voice brought back unto mine ear
The thought which from my doubting eye was hid.

This spark lit up, in vivid hues and clear,
The memory of the sorely changed brow;
Then did Forese to my gaze appear.

"Ah! look not in such wonder on me now,
All dimm'd and pallid as with foul disease,"
He said, "nor at the leanness of my woe;

But truly tell me of thyself, and those
Who go with thee; nor let thy speech be stay'd,
The ardent longing of my soul to ease."

"Thy face, o'er which in death such tears I shed

Of old, now makes me grieve with no less woe,
Because I see it here so marr'd," I said.

First tell, I pray thee, why thy bones thus grow
Unto their covering ; hardly may he speak,
Whose eager mind some wish'd·for thing would know."

He said : " In God's own counsel ye must seek
The virtue to the tree and fountain given,
From whence ye see me now so lean and weak.

Each one who, weeping, sings, is punish'd even
For gluttony ; and therefore thus he grieves,
In thirst and hunger purified for heaven.

To every soul impatient longing cleaves,
From the sweet odour of the fruit, and from
The dash of waters, showering on the leaves.

Not once alone our footsteps hither come,
Our pains renewing : yet it is not pain,
But a sweet comfort sent us from our home.

The tree by that same hill we would attain,
Which erst led Christ with joyful lips to say,
' *Eloi*,' when there flow'd from every vein,

His saving blood." " Forest, from the day,"
I said, "when thou hast gone to better life,

Five years not yet have wholly pass'd away.

If near the ending of thine earthly strife
The strength for aa hath fail'd thee, ere the hour
Which led thee back to God with holy grief,

How to ascend on high hadst thou the power?
Low on the island shore I thee had sought,
Where lapse of time doth time mis-spent restore."

And he to me: "So soon I here was brought,
To drink the cup wherein sweet wormwood lies,
By my own Nella's love, with weeping fraught.

I by her prayers devout, and mournful sighs,
From out the land that is with longing rife
Was drawn; and through each zone had strength to rise.

So much more dear to God is my sweet wife,
Whom erst, while yet I lived, I loved so well,
As there are few like her in her true life.

For the Sardinian land, of which they tell
Such tales, beth citizens more chaste than they
Of the Barbagia where she still doth dwell.

My gentle brother, what then can I say?
Before my inward vision doth appear
A future time, not distant from this day,

Which shall the Church's fulmination bear,
Against the dames of Florence, who go forth,
And on their swelling breasts no covering wear.

Upon what heathen race, on all the earth,
Was it e'er needful, edicts to impose,
That from or Men or Heaven have had their birth,

To clothe them ?   When each shameless woman
    knows
What Heaven's swift circling orbit bears along,
For loudest wail her lips she may unclose.

And if my foresight do not lead me wrong,
This sorrow cometh, ere the beard shall grow
Of him who now is soothed by nursery song.

But hide not from me what I fain would know ;
Not only I, thou seest, but all our band
Gaze where upon the ground no sunbeams glow."

Then I to him : " If thou wouldst call to mind
What thou hast seen with me, and I with thee,
Sad were the memory of thy native land.

I from that life, by him who goes with me,
Was led, the evening before yesternight,
When she, the sister of this orb we see,

Shone in the fullest circle of her light ; "
(And to the Sun I pointed :) " through the land
Of everlasting death he led aright

 My mortal footsteps. Thence did I ascend,
Guided by him, and circling round the hill
Which makes you once again to duty bend.

 To lead me he hath promised, until
I rise where Beatrice doth dwell on high ;
Without him must I there my quest fulfil.

 And this is Virgil, who thus spake," (and I
Towards him pointed) " and this other Shade
Is he for whose ascent unto the sky

 Your kingdom, to its base, the earthquake's might
  obey'd."

CANTO XXIV.

Our speed check'd not our words, nor they more
    slow
Our footsteps made ; but on we swiftly sped,
As ships that driven before fresh breezes go :
    And still those Shades, who seem'd as things twice
      dead,
Gazed through the hollow caverns of their eyes,
In wonder that I yet had life.   I said,
    Continuing my speech : "This soul may rise
More slowly unto Heaven, it well may be,
Even for the cause which in another lies.
    But where Piccarda is, now tell to me ,

And say if some a name of note do bear,
Among the Shades who gaze so fixidly."

"My sister, who was erst so good and fair,
I know not which the most, in the bright ray
Of Paradise her golden crown doth wear."

This first was said; then: "In this some we may
Each name his brother; since, as by disease,
Fell hunger hath our semblance worn away.

This Shade is Buonagiunta, the Lucchese;"
(And, with his hand, towards him made a sign),
"And he whose meagreness doth most displease,

Once Holy Church embraced; he and his line
Erst were of Tours: here is his penance done,
E'en for Bolsena's eels, and dainty wine,

Vernaccia hight." And others, one by one,
He show'd, and to be named was each content,
And sombre looks among them there were none.

There Ubaldin di Pila seem'd intent
Vainly to gnaw with hungry tooth; and there
Was Boniface, to whom on earth was lent

Of many souls the pastoral rule and care.
And him I saw, who erst within Forli,

Drank the good wine with lesser thirst than here,
    And yet therewith ne'er know satiety.
Mine eyes on the Lucchese I now did strain,
More eagerly than on the rest ; and he
    Seem'd that of me like knowledge he would gain.
Gentucca then he murmur'd ; to mine ear
Came the low sound, as dull'd by hunger's pain ;
    And then I said : "O soul, who dost appear
Thus to desire to tell me all thy tale,
Uplift thy voice, that I may rightly hear."

    "A woman now is born who yet no veil
Doth wear," he said, " and she will make thee prize
My city, although men against it rail.
    Go, with this prophecy before thine eyes ;
For if my whisper thee to doubt doth move,
Within the future the fulfilment lies.
    But say, if I the wondrous fortune prove
Of seeing him who in new rhyme hath sung,
Fair ladies who have hearts attuned to love."
    I answer'd : "I in very truth am one
Who when my soul is with love's breathings fraught,
Sing as the thoughts within my heart have sprung."

"O brother, now I see," he said, "the knot
That erst Guittone and the notary kept,
And me, from the sweet music of thy thought.

Well do I see how thy bold pinions swept,
Fast-following the dictator of thy strain,
While ours, in sooth, all tame and powerless slept

And he who to more knowledge would attain,
Sees how apart the new from ancient style,
And to be silent, in content, is fain."

Even as the birds who winter by the Nile,
In flocks oft linger on their onward way,
Then fly, with sudden haste, in a long file ;
~ Thus all those spirits quickly turn'd away,
With footsteps lighter for their frames so lean,
And for the longing that within them lay.

And as the man who hath aweary been
With running, stays his steps, until the haste
And flutterings of his breath be calm'd ; I ween,

Thus did Forese, till the rest were past,
While by my side he journey'd ; then he said :
"When shall I see thee once again at last ?"

I spake : "Now know I not how long my thread

Of life ; yet may I not so soon return,
As to this shore my longing shall be led.

Because the city of my earthly bourne
More barren is of good, from hour to hour,
Seeming as if it, ruin'd, soon should mourn."

He said : " The man whose guilt hath been most sore,
Dragg'd by his horse I ere upon the ground,
Anear the vale whence ye return no more.

His steed more swiftly at each step doth bound ;
On, on, until it strikes the fatal blow,
And vilely mangled, there his corpse is found.

Not many circuits those bright wheels shall know,"
(And heavenward then he glanced) " till that be clear
Which my discourse hath now no power to show

But I must leave thee : for the time is dear,
Within this kingdom ; and too much I lose
In ling'ring for thy slower footsteps here."

As, from the calvacade, a knight doth use
To spur his steed, all eager for the fray,
First to win honour where the red blood flows,

With bounding step from us he pass'd away ;
And I with those two spirits was alone,

Who upon earth were heroes.   When there lay

  Such space between us that my eyes were gone   100

In search of him, as erst my thoughts, intent

To know the things his speech to me had shown,

  I saw another tree, which seemed bent

With the rich fruit that every branch down weigh'd,

Anear ; and tow'rds it now our footsteps went.   105

  And some were there, who, 'neath its heavy shade,

With hands uplifted, spake unto the leaves,

I know not what ; but like a child they pray'd,

  As unto one who yet no answer gives ,

But, to increase the strong desire they bear,   110

Holds that on high for which each spirit grieves.

  Then they depart, with wish ungranted then ;

And onwards to the mighty tree we pass'd,

Which still refuses every tear and prayer.

  " Pass on ; anear this shade ye may not rest .   115

There is a tree above, whence Eve erst took

The fatal apple , this hath the same taste."

  Thus said the boughs some unknown voices spoke ;

And I with Virgil and with Statius sought

To cling more closely to the circling rock.   120

" Remember the accursed creatures brought
From out a shadowy cloud, and drunk with wine,
When Theseus 'gainst their double forces fought.

Think of the Hebrews too, who gave that sign,
The self-indulgent draught, when Gideon's band
Came down to battle against Midian's line."

Those airy spirit-voices, on each hand,
Discoursing thus of gluttony we heard,
The sin wherein sad wages aye attend.

We pass'd along the path, which now appear'd
Uncumber'd, for a thousand steps and more,
And each in moving utter'd not a word.

" What thought on you who journey weighs so sore!"
Was said; whereat I started with affright,
As doth a beast whom sudden fear comes o'er.

I look'd to see what now should meet my sight :
And never, in the furnace' crimson glow,
Shone glass or metal with such fiery light,

As did the radiant form I look'd on now.
He said : " Now turn ye, and the mount ascend,
If ye to everlasting peace would go."

His aspect did my mortal eyesight blind ;

Backward I turn'd, to those my steps who bore
Along, that at their bidding I might wend.

And as, sweet heralds of the dawning hour,
Come the May breezes from the fields of bloom,
All laden with the scent of herb and flower,

Even thus, the floating of the angel-plume
I felt, that for a moment touch'd my face,
Wafting ambrosial breath of rich perfume.

And then I heard : " Blessèd is he whom grace
Illumines, so that love of dainty food
Within his heart should hold a measured place ,

Nor dim the light of reason with its vapours rude "

CANTO XXV.

—•—

Argument

Ascent to the Seventh Circle —Discourse of Statius.

Now was the hour that hath no time of rest :
For noon had shone, and the fierce solar ray
Had Taurus left ; and night the Scorpion pass'd.

  And therefore, as the man who doth not stay,
But journeys on, whate'er he chance to see,
Such needful haste impels him on his way ;

  Not with less ardent longing then did we,
Each following each, the upward path begin,
Parted, because so near its ramparts be.

  As the young bird that in the air would spring,
Eager for flight, and yet is not content
To leave the nest, but folds again its wing ;

Even so was I, with wish lit up and spent,
Ere I could frame the question ; and, at last,
I seem'd as one who on discourse is bent.

My gentle father, though in eager haste,
Stay'd not his words, but said : " Now mayst thou speed
The dart which thou upon the cord dost rest."

Then gladly was my prison'd longing freed ,
I spake : " How may they be so wan and lean,
Here, where of nourishment they have no need ? "

If Meleager thou of old hadst seen,
Consuming with the burning of a brand,"
He said, " this unto thee more plain had been.

And if within thee thou couldst understand
How in the mirror thine own form doth glide,
Less hard should be the manner of this land.

But, that by thee this may be well deserted,
Lo ! here is Statius , I to him will pray
That he be thy physician and thy guide."

" If I eternal truth before him lay,"
Thus Statius spake, " may my request be heard
For pardon that I cannot say thee nay."

Then he continued : " If my every word,

N 2

My son, within thy memory thou wilt keep,

That shall be light which darkness erst appear'd.

   Know, the most perfect life, which doth not creep

Along each artery, but still remains

As food uneaten, in the heart doth reap

   Virtue informative, as through the veins,

Still flowing in its destined stream, the root

Its pristine strength and purity regains.

   Then of its onward course perchance 'twere best

That I were silent ; yet I surely deem

The breath of God on earthly life hath pass'd.

   A spirit sheds forth its creative beam

On leaves and flowers of every diverse hue,

This by the wayside, that along the stream :

   Even so, it doth each living thing imbue,

First with the duller life that on the shore

Through the sea-fungus creeps ; and then anew,

   Organic force developes.   Here once more,

My son, the hidden strength thou well mayst know,

Whence nature doth produce her ample store.

   But whence the spring of nobler life may flow

Thou dost not yet behold : this is the point

Which hath bewilder'd wiser men than thou.

And in their doctrine they have oft disjoin'd
The soul from possible intellect, because
It seems no outward organ to appoint

Now ope thy mind unto the eternal laws
Of truth ; and know, that, when the infant brain
Unto its full articulation grows,

Then the great Mover turns to it, and fain,
Breathes over Nature's work the living mind, .
The spirit which much virtue doth contain,

Whereby, when it in substance is combined,
It forms a conscious, individual soul,
A sentient life, of that which it doth find.

And lest too marvellous to thee be all
My words, behold the sun, which turns to wine
The juice that from the ripen'd grape doth fall.

When Lachesis hath wholly spun her line,
The spirit then is freed from fleshly root,
And with it bears the human and divine.

Each sensual power remains mort and mute ;
But memory, intellect, and will are now
In act, much more than at the first, acute.

It tarrieth not, but of itself doth go
To one or other of the streams of death ;
Then knows if it shall rise or sink below.

Soon as the soul its destined dwelling hath,
Again shines forth the strength from which it drew
Its life, when in the land of mortal breath.

And as ye see, when watery mists imbue
Our atmosphere, the sunny rays appear
Therein reflected, in each diverse hue ;

Thus doth the soul an airy semblance wear,
Which is in outward limbs and shape the same
Impression, which the inward seal doth bear

And as the fire is follow'd by the flame,
So its new form the spirit must pursue,
And this aërial body hath its name

Of Shade, because its movements ever show
The soul within ; and thus may we, the while,
Each feeling prove which on the earth we knew.

Therefore we speak, and therefore do we smile ,
And from this source the tears and plaints arise,
Which thou hast heard along thy path of toil.

By that whereon the strong affection lies,

The outward shape is fashion'd; thus ye see
The cause of what ye look'd on with surprise."

Now to the last abode of torture, we
Had come; and to the right hand then we turn'd,
And bent on other cares our thoughts must be: 105

For here, with fiercest flames the rampart burn'd,
And from the ledge a whistling wind is sent,
That blows them back; whence I a path discern'd.

Thus, one by one, along the verge we went,
And there the fire did surely me astray,   110
And here I dreaded the unveil'd descent

My Leader said to me: "Upon this way,
Needs must ye keep the bridle on your eyes;
Because, in sooth, ye easily may stray."

"O God, in whom all grace and mercy lies,"   115
From out the bosom of the fiery glow
Was sung; whereat I turn'd me, in surprise.

For Shades amid the flame pass'd to and fro;
Then on my steps and their's I fix'd my gaze,
Now here, now there, alternating   And lo!   120

When they had sung what there the Psalmist says,
They, "*Virum non cognosco*," cried aloud;

Then, in low voice, repeat the hymn of praise.

And, ending, they went on: "Within the wood
Diana dwelt, and chased the nymph away,
Of old, who Venus' power had not withstood."

Then they again resumed the sacred lay ;
And told of those who during life were pure,
In nuptial bonds.   And, in this manner, they

Discourse and sing, the while their pains endure ;
Till they this some of burning flame have past :
For with such discipline they needs must cure

The wound of sin, that shall be fully heal'd at last.

CANTO XXVI.

Argument.

The Seventh Circle.—Dante speaks with Guido Guinicelli, the
Florentian, and Arnault, the Provençal Troubadour.

WHILE, one by one, we pass'd along this bourne,
Full oft to me my gentle guide did say :
" Beware ; for it is well I thee should warn."

On my right shoulder now the sunbeams lay,
And shed their splendour over all the west,
Changing the azure to a golden ray.

And, for the darkness by my form imprest
Upon the path, still brighter was the gleam ;
Thus many look'd toward me, as they pass'd.

Thus was the cause for which, I surely deem,
They now began to speak of me, and said :
" In sooth, no form aerial doth he seem "

And then as near me, in their course, they sped,
As well might be while heedful still to go
Where the red flames their burning ardour shed.

"O thou, who go'st with footsteps not more slow,
But rev'rently still following thy guide,
Reply to me, here parching in fierce glow.

Nor I alone thine answer do abide :
All these have greater thirst for thy reply
Than hath the Indian for the cooling tide.

Then tell us why on thee the sunbeams lie,
Nor do they pass beyond thy form ; as though
Thou wert of those whose lot is still to die."

Thus one among them spake to me ; and now
Would I have answer'd him, but swiftly came
Before me somewhat new and strange : for lo !

Even in the middle of the path of flame,
A band who, coming tow'rd us, onward press'd .
That sight my silent thought did wholly claim

And as the spirits drew anear, with haste
Each folded each within a brief embrace ;
And then pass'd on, content with scanty feast :

Even so the ants' small, dusky insect race

A moment meet in their industrious art,
Perchance their fortune and their ways to trace.

When from the friendly greeting they depart,
Ere yet one step had each from each pass'd by,
Some, with loud, emulous voices, from the heart

Bewail, and "Sodom and Gomorrah!" cry;
And, "Bear ye still in mind the sins which are
Told in Pasiphae's tale," the rest reply.

Even as the cranes, that tow'rd the Northern Star
In part do fly, part to the desert-sand;
And these from frost, and those from sun are far:

So do they come and go, on either hand,
And, weeping, turn again to their first song,
And to the cry most suited to their band.

Then, they who first address'd me in the throng
Again toward me turn'd, with eager mien,
As they to list to my discourse did long

And I, who, twice, their strong desire had seen,
My speech began: "Ye souls, who are secure,
One day, to dwell 'mid heavenly pastures green,

Know, that my limbs, nor youthful nor mature,
In earth not yet are buried, but I still

With living flesh and blood my toil endure.

To cure my blinded eyes I climb this hill
There is a lady in the realms above ;
And I, a mortal, by her aid fulfil

My quest in this your world.   As ye would prove
The gladness soon of the empyrial heaven,
Whose ample spaces are all fill'd with love,

Say, (for perchance to me it shall be given
To tell the tale,) who ye may be, and those
Who speed, and to another goal are driven ?"

Not more amaze the mountain-peasant shows,
In silent wonder, all uncouth and rude,
When first he to the polish'd city goes,

Than did these Shades who now, astonish'd, stood ;
But quickly did that stupor pass away,
Which lasts not long in hearts of lofty mood.

Then he who first address'd me 'gan to say :
" Blessed be thou, who journeyest to win
Experience which on earth may guide thy way.

Know, that the sun of these the same hath been
As Cæsar's, whence in his triumphal hour
The soldiers, in contempt, proclaim'd him Queen.

Therefore they name the city which, of yore,
Was with that crime defiled, and with their shame
They lend the scorching furnace fiercer power.

Our sin was of another stamp and name:
But, since the laws of reason we pass'd by,
And even degraded as brute beasts became,

Thus, in our own reproof, we loudly cry,
And tell of her who, in the Cretan clime,
Was erst most beastly in vile luxury.

Our actions now thou knowest, and our crime:
If of our earthly names thou wouldst enquire,
To tell of all thou seest, there lacketh time.

Yet, of myself I answer thy desire:
I Guido Guinicelli was, ere death,
Repentance caused me heavenward to aspire"

As, 'mid the fury of Lycurgus' wrath,
The sons toward their mournful mother sprang,
Even so did I, soon as I heard the breath,

Revealing him whose voice melodious rang
So sweet, that I and wiser poets learn'd
Of him the lovely strain which erst he sang.

And, lost in silent thought, full oft I turn'd,

Looking on him, whom yet I might not reach,
For the fierce flame which from the rampart burn'd.

Then fill'd with gazing, did I him beseech
That he his heart's desire to me would tell,
And with a sacred promise seal'd my speech.

And he to me : "Such memories aye shall dwell
Within me of thy words, that Lethe's stream
Their clearness may not darken or dispel

But, if thou speak'st as truly as I deem,
Now tell me wherefore, in discourse and gaze,
So loving unto me thou still dost seem ?"

And I to him : "Because of thy sweet lays,
Which long as modern use its power doth hold,
Shall win from men the meed of lofty praise."

He said : "My brother, he whom yo behold"
(And tow'rds another then he turn'd his glance)
"More nobly did his native language mould ;

For, in love-poesy and prose-romance,
He bore the palm ; despite the fools who say
The Limousin before him did advance.

By fame, much more than fact, do men alway
Guide their belief ; and thus decide, before

Or reason or experience lead the way.

    Thus they exalted, in the days of yore,
Only Guittone, with applauding cry,
Till truth, with their false praise, they downward bore

    Now, if such grace is given, that thou mayst try
The journey to the heavenly cloister, where
Christ rules the brotherhood who dwell on high,

    I beg, that thou for me wouldst say the prayer
He taught, as far as we have need who dwell
Where we can sin no more."   He said ; and there

    Gave place to him of whom he erst did tell,
And disappear'd amid the burning flame,
As doth a fish within its watery cell.

    To him whom he had shown me, then I came
A little nearer ; and I begg'd that he
Unto my longing would make known his name.

    He thus began, with gracious mien and free :
" So sweet to me thy courteous questioning,
Nor can nor will I hide thy wish from thee

    I am Arnaut, who mourn the while I sing ;
Sadly I look upon my folly past,
And joyful, on the bliss that Heaven shall bring.

I pray thee, by the virtue which at last
Shall guide thee where there is nor heat nor cold,
There on my pain a thought of pity cast."

He ceased; and once again the fire did him enfold.

CANTO XXVII.

Argument.

At the name of Beatrice, Dante passes through the flames of
the seventh and last circle of Purgatory.—In a vision, he
sees Leah, the symbol of active life.

As when the earliest radiance of the sun
Dawns where its Maker shed his sacred blood,
And 'neath the midnight Ebro flows adown,

   And noonday burns above the Ganges' flood,
Thus was it now; and daylight sank, before
God's holy angel in our presence stood,

   And joyful sang beside the fiery shore
" *Beati mundo corde,*" in a strain
Far sweeter than ye find in mortal lore.

   " Ye blessed ones, until the fiery pain
Have touch'd you, ye may seek no onward way .
Enter; nor turn ye from the heavenly plain,

Whence cometh to your ears that lovely lay."
These words he spake, as we to him drew near;
And I became like one whose burial-day

Is come, though yet in life. My hands, in fear,
I stretch'd, and gazed upon the flame, and thought
Of those whom I had seen on fiery bier.

Then both my friends came tow'rds me, as I sought
Their glance, and Virgil said to me: " My son,
This flame with torment, not with death, is fraught

Remember thee, remember—and if aons
Might hurt, when I on Geryon was thy guide,
Why fearest now, when nearer to God's throne !

Be sure, that if within yon fiery tide
Thou for a thousand years and more shouldst dwell,
Thou couldst not lose a hair from off thy head.

If thou dost doubt the thing whereof I tell,
And by experience certainty would gain,
Thou with thy garment mayst thy fears dispel

No more let cowardice thy steps detain ;
But turn and cross the path which yonder lies."
Yet, 'gainst my conscience, still I did remain.

This when he saw, a cloud pass'd o'er his eyes,

And anxiously, " Behold, my son," he said,
" Twixt thee and Beatrice this wall doth rise."

As Pyramus, when death toward him sped,
Yet oped once more his eyes at Thisbe's name,
What time the mulberry was stain'd with red,

All pliant then my stubborn mood became ;
And to my Leader, when I heard the sound
Which told of her so dearly loved, I came.

And then he shook his head, and spake : " This
    bound
Thou fain wouldst pass ? "   And gently did he smile,
As to a child who all subdued is found,

By promised toy.   He led me on the while,
Within the flame, and begg'd that Statius now
Would follow, who for many a bygone mile

Had parted us.   So fierce the fiery glow,
That soothing, molten glass, compared with this,
Were as a grot where crystal waters flow.

And then, to cheer my failing heart, I wis,
My gentle father, mid that raging heat,
Spake but of Beatrice, and said : " In hbhs

I see her shining eyes."   And now a sweet

Clear voice of singing floated to mine ear,
And led us where the shore our steps did greet.

"Come, blessed of my Father," did I hear,
In melody, within a starry ray
Of light too pure for mortal eyes to bear.

"Now swiftly comes the closing hour of day:
Ye may not linger here, but onward press,
Ere from the west the sunset fades away."

Between the stony ramparts did we pass,
So that on me the dying light was thrown,
Which slowly sank, as though in weariness.

And but a little way our steps had gone;
When, by the shadowy form effaced, we knew
That darkness fell where erst the sunbeams shone.

Ere the horizon changed its varied hue,
Unto the dimness of the twilight gray,
And night, o'er all, her dusky mantle threw,

Each on a grade of the steep staircase lay,
And there we made our couch; because all power
For the ascent departeth with the day.

Even as the flock, at the fierce noontide hour,
Quietly repose within the stilly shade,

Though where the peaks of the high mountains soar
   Erst with bold leap they sprang, they now are laid
To rest, and slowly ruminate, and still
Their pastor leaning on his staff is stay'd,
   And aye his faithful task he doth fulfil,
And ever the lone midnight watch doth keep,
Lest wolves may cause his charge or fear or ill;
   Thus were we now: I, as the timid sheep,
And they, as shepherds guarding me by night,
Enfolded in the ramparts strait and steep.
   Small was the space beyond, which met my sight,
But, in that little, I the stars beheld
Shining with larger orbs and purer light.
   And still I gazed upon the glittering field,
And mused, till slumber came, and seal'd mine eye,
Slumber, wherein the truth is oft reveal'd.
   Now, in the hour when in the orient sky
The star of Venus dawns with silver beam,
Where love's soft radiance ever glows on high,
   A young and beauteous lady, in a dream
To me appear'd, as through a flowery plain
She went, and cull'd the blossoms, whose bright gleam

Bedeck'd the grass; and thus she sang her strain:
"Know, I am Leah; and throughout this bourne
I go, and weave a blooming garland fain,

And at this mirror I myself adorn.
But never doth my sister Rachel gaze
Within that glass; she sitteth, night and morn,

With eye intent upon the holy rays
That shine around the glories of God's throne:
To her, of thought; to me, of work the praise."

Now, from the splendours that precede the dawn,
More grateful to the wand'ring pilgrim's eye
Than home, when he a weary way hath gone,

On every side the clouds of darkness fly,
And with them fled my slumber; then I rose,
And saw my Master prompt the path to try.

"That sweetest fruit, which on such diverse boughs
The anxious care of mortals eye doth seek,
To-day shall lull in peace thy many woes."

Thus did I hear my gentle Leader speak,
And never such deep joy to me was given,
As in those welcome words I here did take;

And thus my will by such strong will was driven,

I seem'd more lightly at each step to go,
And with first pinions might ascend to heaven.

As the whole staircase we surmounted now,
And stood at last upon the grade supern,
Then Virgil fix'd his gaze upon my brow,

And said: "The temporal fire and the etern
Thou hast beheld, my son; and, from this day,
The truth by me no more thou shalt discern.

I led thee when thou wert gone far astray;
Now, thine own pleasure thou mayst take as guide:
Thou art beyond the steep and narrow way.

Behold the sun, that on thy brow doth glide;
Behold each flower which on thy pathway lies,
Sprung from the bounteous earth, on every side:

Until there come to thee the lovely eyes
That, weeping, bade me and thee, it is thine
Freely to rest, and freely to arise.

No longer tarry for my speech or sign;
For now thy heart is righteous, pure, and just,
Nor unto evil things canst thou incline:

Thus, to thy will, both crown and mitre I entrust."

CANTO XXVIII.

Argument.

The terrestrial Paradise.--Matilda.

EAGER to roam the forest-depths divine
Of thick and living foliage, whose rich gloom
Temper'd the dawn unto my mortal eyne,

I linger'd not, but through the flowery bloom,
Leaving the shore, I went with paces slow
Amid the herbage fraught with sweet perfume.

A pleasant air that seem'd no change to know,
Smote on my forehead with soft motion, still
As gentle as when summer breezes blow.

And then the leaves which, ever trembling, thrill,
With one accord all bent toward the part
Where fell the shadow of the holy hill.

Yet not thereby so far did they depart
From the sweet calmness of this sunny clime,
That the small birds should cease them from their art;

But the fresh breathings of the hour of prime,
Singing, they gladly welcomed 'mong the leaves,
Which kept low murmuring tune unto their rhyme:

Even as from bough to bough the ear perceives,
In the pine-forest near to Chiassi's shore,
A melody when the east wind receives

Behest from Eolus.   My footsteps bore
Me slowly onward through the ancient wood,
Until the entrance I beheld no more;

And lo! my path was ended, where a flood
Towards the left did with soft ripple glide,
Bending the grass that on its margin stood.

Here, even the purest and most crystal tide
Yet somewhat dull'd with earthly taint would seem,
Near this, which nought within its depths might hide;

Though in the dusky twilight doth its stream
Pass 'neath perpetual shadow, where there lies
Nor golden sun nor moonlight's silver beam.

My footsteps here were stay'd; but with mine eyes

I pass'd beyond the river, to admire
The fresh May-garlands' green diversities:

   And then appear'd, as that which doth inspire
Most sudden marvel, and within thy thought
Doth leave no other fancy nor desire,

   A lady singing all alone, who sought
Amid the field of flowers each fairest flower,
Wherewith on every side her path was fraught.

   "Ah! beauteous lady, who in this sweet hour
Dost seem to bask within love's radiance clear,
If semblance to reveal the heart have power,"

   I said, "now of thy courtesy draw near,
That the melodious song which thou dost sing
May come more plainly to my list'ning ear.

   Thou dost unto my thought the memory bring
Of Proserpine, when her sad mother lost
Her smile, and she the gladness of the spring."

   At these my words she turn'd towards me fast,
As one who dances with swift footsteps light,
Scarcely I saw her moving, while she pass'd

   Above the blooms of gold and crimson bright,
And low unto the earth her eyes she bent,

As maiden who would shrink from human sight.

But yet did she my eager prayers content,
And drew so near, that her sweet melodies
With clearest meaning to my ear were sent ;

And when she came to where the herbage bus
Bathed in the waters of the lovely stream,
Full courteously to me she raised her eyes :

I well believe that with such radiant beam
The orbs of Venus shone not, when of yore
Pierced by her son.   Then smiled with sunny gleam

The maiden, as she stood upon the shore,
Wreathing the flowers that in this lofty land
The soil without or seed or culture bore.

But little space was 'twixt each river-strand :
Yet Hellespont, where Xerxes cross'd the strait,
(Which still as curb to human pride doth stand,)

Ne'er from Leander suffer'd such deep hate,
Where Sestos and Abydos by the wild
Sea waves are parted, as from me this gate.

Thus she began : " Perchance because I smiled,
Ye who are strangers in this place, elect
For man, as is the cradle for the child,

May somewhat, in your wond'ring thought, suspect;
But where the Psalmist *Delectasti* said
Shall clearly shine upon thine intellect.

And thou, who go'st before, and me hast pray'd
To speak, what wouldst thou know? for I am bound
To answer thee, till thy desire be stay'd."

I spake: " The river and the woodland sound
Impugn within me, by a newer faith,
The first reply which to my quest I found."

And she: " Now tell I thee the thing which hath
So strange a semblance; and thereby shall cease
The darkness of the clouds which hide thy path.

God, who is glad in his own blessedness,
Created man unsinning; and this land
Gave him as earnest of eternal peace.

By his own fault full soon did he descend,
By his own fault, in mourning and in woe
He did his sinless smiles and joyance end.

But know, that lest the stormy winds which blow,
Raised by the mists that come from earth and sea,
The mists which in the sun's warm footsteps go,

Should here some cause of hurt or hindrance be,

This mountain-top ascends so near to heaven,
And of such strife is, from its portal, free.

And, as in circuit all the air is driven,
Revolving with the first ethereal sphere,
If by no jutting point some stay be given ;

Thus, on this height, that floateth in the clear
And living air, its motion strikes, and thence
Arise the woodland whispers which ye hear.

Such virtue dwelleth in this forest dense,
The rowith it penetrates the air around,
Which, ever circling, sheds its burden hence.

For even upon the lower world is found
A diff'rent climate beneath varying skies,
And diverse plants proceed from diverse ground :

And, hearing this, it causeth not surprise,
When some wild plant or herb, at its own will,
Without or seed or culture, doth arise.

And thou shouldst know, that all this holy hill,
Where now thou art, is full of every seed
And fruit that springeth not on earth.   The rill,

Which here thou lookest on, doth not proceed
From source replenished by rain or snows,

As rivers which of fresh supplies have need ;

But from a full and certain fount it flows,
Which by God's will is with so much imbued,
Wherewith it in diverging courses goes.

Toward us, on this side, descends a flood,
That bears away the memory of thy sin ;
The other gives thee back again each good.

This stream is Lethe ; where the waves begin
Thence to depart, flows down Eunoe's rill :
By tasting both, their virtue thou shalt win.

Their wave all other savours doth excel ;
And though thy thirst might well be sated even
Did I no more discourse with thee, yet still

A corollary shall, of grace, be given ;
Nor shall it less be prized, I surely deem,
If more than promised be my words of heaven.

Those who, of ancient times, in the bright gleam
Of Poesy beheld the age of gold,
Perchance in high Parnassus had this dream.

Here man was innocent, in days of old ;
Here, ays in autumn and eternal spring ;
This is the nectar of which erst they told."

Towards the Poets now, with eager wing,
My glances sped, and saw the smile which came,
Soon as they heard this last imagining;

Then once again I turn'd unto that fairest dame.

CANTO XXIX.

— ◆ —

Argument.

The three poets pursue their way along the bank of the stream
—Apocalyptic visions.

As one enamour'd, singing a sweet lay,
She ended thus her fair discourse, and said :
" Blessèd is he whose sins are purged away."

Like nymphs who stray amid the sylvan shade,
Alone, and now they seek the sunny beam,
Now of its burning light are they afraid,

Thus did she bend her course, against the stream,
Still wand'ring on the flowery bank ; and I,
As her slow steps, went slowly.   And, I deem,

Not yet a hundred paces did we try,
'Twixt hers and mine, when lo ! the streamlet roll'd
Toward the shining of the eastern sky

Nor long we thus our onward way did hold,

When the fair maiden turn'd to me, and said :

" My brother, look and listen."   And behold !

A sudden splendour o'er the forest shed

Brightness amid the glooms from every part ;

I deem'd, perchance the lightning's flash had sped

But not as lightning did the gleam depart ;

It brighten'd more unto the perfect morn :

" What thing is this !" I said within my heart.

And a sweet voice of melody was borne

Upon the luminous air , and then mine ire

Rose against Eve, because with daring scorn,

When earth obey'd, and the bright heavenly quire,

A woman, new-created, all alone

Lifted the veil that hid our knowledge dire .

Else had I never made so sad a moan ;

And those delights ineffable, I wis,

Long years ago for aye I should have known.

While 'mid such earnests of eternal bliss

I went, and still more eagerly did long

For fuller glimpses of the land of peace,

I saw amid the green and tangled throng

Of forest leaves, it seem'd, a burning fire,

And then I knew that the sweet sound was song.

　O holy, holiest maidens of the lyre,

If ever, for your sakes, on me hath lain

Hunger, or cold, or vigils, I require

　My guerdon.　Let Urania's starry train

Give of the fount of Helicon, that I

Strong thoughts may render into measured strain.

　A little further on did I descry

Somewhat ; it seem'd, seven trees of gold, methought ;

Because much space 'twixt them and me did lie

　But when I near this wond'rous sight was brought,

No more did faint resemblance do me wrong,

Nor distance longer with deceit was fraught.

　And I perceived, in truthful reason strong,

What seem'd as trees were lamps of golden light,

And heard *Hosanna* in the voice of song

　On high, resplendent shone this radiance bright,

More clear than moon in the blue depths serene,

In her mid month at middle hour of night.

　Admiring much at this strange thing, I ween,

To Virgil then I turn'd, and he replied

To me, with no less wonder in his mien.

I look'd once more tow'rds that which I descried,
The vision which advanced with paces slow,
More tardy than of newly-wedded bride   60

The lady spake . " Now wherefore dost thou glow
Thus in the aspect of yon living flame,
Nor seek'st the thing which follows it to know ?"

Then saw I those who in white garments came,
Following their leader's steps , no living wight   66
Hath seen such snowy gleam.   And with the same

Full splendour did the stream give back the light,
And there as plainly did my form appear,
As though a spotless mirror met my sight.

When to the river's brink I drew so near,   70
That but the stream before me I might find,
I stopp'd to look upon the radiance clear.

And now the flames advance, and leave behind
A trail of glory, painting all the air,
Like bright-hued banners borne upon the wind.   75

Seven diverse bands within the splendour were ,
Of the same hues from which the Sun his bow
Doth form, the Moon her silver girdle fair

More distant than my mortal sight might know
They stream'd beyond the far horizon's bound;
In breadth, I think, ten paces ye might go.

And, 'neath the light their splendours shed around,
Lo! twice twelve elders, twain by twain, drew nigh;
Each with a lily diadem was crown'd.

And they their voices lifted up on high,
And sang: "Among Eve's daughters thou art blest,
And blessed be thy loveliness for aye."

After this band of souls elect had pass'd,
Nor longer were the flowers and herbage green,
Beyond the streamlet, by their footsteps prest,

As light succeeding light on high is seen,
Four living creatures in their traces came,
Their brows enwreathed with freshest leaves, I ween.

And each six pinions bore : in hue the same,
Gemm'd with such eyes as Argus had of yore,
But shining with a yet more living flame.

It needs not now that I should linger more,
And spend my rhymes in telling of their form,
Because I now must turn to other lore.

But if therewith thou wouldst thy mind inform,

Read in Ezekiel, from the land of cold
How they came forth in lightning and in storm

  The vision on his page thou dost behold,
Thus here; save that St. John saw not the same,
Touching their plumes, but with me doth hold.   105

  Within the space those creatures did enframe,
A chariot borne upon triumphal wheels,
And harness'd to a flying griffin, came.

  In such a wise this wond'rous stud reveals
His wings between the bands of rainbow light,   110
That none of their bright beauty he conceals.

  Those pinions rose beyond my mortal sight:
And glittering gold the plumage that they wore;
All else, vermilion, tinging snowy white.

  Never did Rome such chariot, of yore,   115
On Scipio or on Cæsar's self bestow:
Yea, by its side the Car of Light were poor,

  The Sun's own car, that burn'd with fiery glow,
When Jove, in hidden justice, heard the cry
Which to his throne from trembling Earth did go   120

  At the right wheel, three damsels seem'd to fly,
With dancing steps   the first so rosy red,

Scarcely in flame ye might her form descry;

The next, who with light motion swiftly sped,
Seem'd wholly radiant with the emerald's glance;
The third appear'd as snow but newly shed.

And now the white-robed maiden led the dance,
Now she of rosy hue; and at her song,
More swift or slow their paces did advance.

And by the left wheel then four pass'd along,
In purple robes; and she their steps who led
Saw with three visual orbs.   Anear this throng,

I saw two ancient men, in garb array'd
Which all unlike in form and hue did seem;
Yet were they like in their demeanour staid.

One seem'd to be a follower of him,
The great Hippocrates, whom nature gave
To those of whom she did most fondly deem.

With contrary intent, a burnish'd glaive
Of sharp and glittering light the other held;
Wherefore I trembled, e'en beyond the wave.

Then four, in humble garments, I beheld;
And following them, came an old man alone,
In slumber, yet with wakeful brow unquell'd.

And all the seven, as those who first had gone,
Were in like raiment cloth'd ; save that, in room
Of lily-blossoms, round their foreheads shone
  Garlands of roses and each crimson bloom :
Well might ye deem, when gazing from afar,
Their burning brows lit up the forest-gloom.

  And when anear me came that wond'rous car,
The thunder spake ; and all the goodly band,
(As though some high behest their way did bar)
  With the seven golden lamps, stood on the river
    strand.

CANTO XXX

Argument

Descent of Beatrice —The Shade of Virgil disappears.—
Statius remains.

When the seven stars of Paradise on high,
That ever with unwaning splendour burn,
Where never cloud, save that of sin, doth lie,

   The stars which here make each his duty learn,
(As lower constellations guide aright
The sailor who his bark would homeward turn,)

   Stay'd in their course, the band in garments white,
Who 'twixt the winged steed and them pass'd by,
Turn'd to the chariot, as to their delight.

   One sang, who seem'd an angel from on high,
" Come, spouse, from Lebanon ;" these words did spring
Thrice from his lips, and thrice the rest reply.

As, when the sound of the last trump shall ring,
The bless'd, rising from their shadowy bourne,
With voice regain'd shall Hallelujah sing;

Thus, on the car divine did I discern
A hundred forms: and but one voice was found
'Mong those bright messengers of life etern.

They "*Benedictus*" sang, and all around
They flung sweet flowers upon the blooming lawn,
And "Give rich wealth of lilies" did resound

Thus have I seen, at hour of dewy dawn,
A rosy flush upon the orient sky,
And o'er the rest serenest azure drawn,

When on the sun's bright face a veil doth lie,
So that upon its soft and temper'd light,
Long ye may gaze with an unwearied eye;

Even thus, within a cloud of blossoms bright,
That, rising from those hands angelic, came,
And fell around the chariot, in my sight,

With snow-white veil and olive diadem,
A Lady I beheld, 'neath mantle green,
Cloth'd in the colour of the living flame.

And then my spirit, which so long had been

Without the trembling thrill her presence bore
Afar into its inmost depths, I ween,

  Although mine eyes reveal'd to me no more,
Yet, moved as by some hidden virtue's sway,
Of ancient love felt once again the power.

  And now, when on my brow once more there lay
The subtle light which o'er my soul was shed,
Ere yet I had come forth from boyhood's day,

  Unto my Comforter I would have sped,
As doth the child unto his mother turn,
When he is grieved, or when he is afraid;

  Thus had I spoken: "Every vein doth burn,
With drops which flow not in a measured tide;
The signs of that old passion I discern."

  But Virgil was no longer by my side,
Virgil, my gentlest friend and father dear,
Virgil, to whom I yielded as my guide;

  Nor all the joys of Paradise, that here
Were shower'd, erst by our earliest mother lost,
Might yet avail to check the flowing tear.

  "Dante, that Virgil from thy side hath past,
Yet weep not, this thou mayst not weep for yet;

Another wound should make thy tears flow fast."

　As admiral, who on the prow is set,
That he, beholding, may give heart to them
Who toil in other ships, even so there met

　My glance (as at the sound of my own name,
Which here must of necessity be told,
I turn'd) upon the chariot's outer frame,

　The Lady whom at first I did behold
Veil'd by the angelic feast, on me did rest
Her gaze beyond where the fair streamlet roll'd.

　Although the veil which bound her forehead, prest
By the dim leaves of Pallas, to mine eye
Caused that her form not yet was manifest,

　Thus did she speak, in regal majesty,
As one who holdeth his discourse, I wis,
While yet a sharper word doth hidden lie :

　"Look on me well ; for I am Beatrice :
How wert thou worthy to attain this mount ?
Dost thou not know that here man dwells in bliss ?"

　Mine eyes sank downwards to the crystal fount ,
But, there beholding me, the herbage green
I sought : such heavy shame downweigh'd my front.

Even thus, the mother wears a haughty mien
Unto her child; because of bitter taste
Is aye that virtue high and harsh, I ween.

She ceased; and suddenly the angel-host
Thus sang: "*Speravi, Domine, in te;*"
And stopp'd, nor beyond "*pedes mios*" pass'd.

As, on the living rafters which there be
In Apennine, the flakes of frozen snow
Are heap'd by winds from the Slavonian sea,

Then melt, and slowly drop from bough to bough,
(When breath'd on by the land whereon there lies
No shadow,) even as wax in fiery glow:

Thus did I stay, without or tears or sighs,
Until they sang the strain whose notes ye find
In music of the ever-moving skies;

And in the song I heard their courteous mind
Of pity for my woe, as though they said:
"Lady, why unto him art so unkind?"

And then the frost, which on my heart was laid,
Melted in vapour and a briny flood,
And from my lips and from my eyes was shed.

She on the chariot-front yet stedfast stood,

Nor from her rigid purpose turn'd away,

But answer'd thus those souls of gentle mood :

  " Ye aye keep watch in the eternal day ;

Nor night nor sleep from you doth ever hide

One footstep made by Time upon his way :   105

  Thus in my answer doth more care abide,

To reach the heart of him who there doth mourn,

That guilt and grief may move in measured tide.

  Not only gifted by the circling bournes,

That leadeth each upon his doomed line,   110

Even with the light his natal star hath worn ;

  But, by the fulness of the grace divine,

(A rain that falls from such high clouds, in sooth,

We may not soar to them with mortal eyne),

  This man was such, in time of early youth,   115

That all high thoughts and habitudes of good

In him full well might have shown forth their truth

  But aye so much more savage and more rude

Is land uncultured, or with seeds of ill,

As it the more with vigour is imbued.   120

  Awhile my presence all his heart did fill,

What time I look'd on him with youthful eye,

And in the true path led him with me still.

    Soon as I touch'd the threshold which doth lie

Between our first existence and our prime,

He turn'd from me to others : when on high

    I rose, a spirit, from the garb of time,

And unto purer, lovelier life I grew,

To him I was less dear.   And in the slime

    Of sin he walk'd through darksome ways untrue,

And sought the lying images of good,

That render not again the promise due.

    Nor did there aught avail with which I would,

By inspiration that in dreams doth lie,

Have call'd him back , so careless was his mood

    And he unto his ruin drew so nigh,

All argument was weak to give him aid,

Saving to show to him the lost for aye

    Thus came I to the portals of the dead ;

And to the Shade who here his steps hath brought,

My prayers, with weeping intermingled, sped.

    The high decrees of God were brought to nought,

If Lethe might be pass'd, and its sweet rill

Be tasted of, without one bitter thought

    Of that repentance which sad tears so well fulfil "

CANTO XXXI.

—•—

Argument.

Dante, having confessed his errors, is bathed by Matilda in
Lethe.—Beatrice unveils.

"O THOU who art beyond the sacred stream,"
(And now towards me the sharp point she bent
Of that discourse whose edge so keen did seem,

And thus she spoke, with voice unhesitant,)
"Say, if this thing be true ; for, when accused,
Herewith thine own confession must be blent."

But all too sorely was my mind confused ;
I would have answer'd ; but the accents died,
Because my voice to form the sound refused

She paused ; then said : "What thoughts in thee abide ?
Answer ; for all thy heart's sad memory
Not yet is wash'd away in Lethe's tide."

Fear and confusion mingled caused that I
Shaped with my lips a " Yes," whose silent speech
More plain to sight than hearing made reply.

Even as a bow, that ye too tightly stretch,
Until it shatters, and, with weaken'd power,
The arrow doth the distant target reach ;

So, 'neath the heavy burden that I bore,
I broke forth in a flood of tears and sighs,
And all my words were lost in sadness sore.

Whence she to me : " What turn'd away thine eyes
From love of the true good, wherein I fain
Had led thee where thou couldst no higher rise ?

What gulf impassable, or what strong chain
Didst find, of power to hinder thus thy feet,
That of the onward path thy hope should wane ?

And what allurement, or what promise sweet,
Upon the brow of others didst descry,
That thou to follow them shouldst be so fleet ?"

And then I drew a long and bitter sigh,
So sad, in sooth, my voice had well nigh fail'd,
And scarce my lips might utter the reply.

Weeping I said : " The things of earth prevail'd,

Deluding me with joys wherein doth dwell
No truth, whene'er from me thy face was veil'd."

"If thou hadst hidden what thou now dost tell,"
She said, "yet still were manifest no less
Thy guilt; there is a Judge who knows it well.

But when with thine own mouth thou dost confess
Thine every sinful deed and grievous wrong,
Backwards the wheel against the blade doth press.

Yet, that a deeper sorrow may belong
Unto thine errors, and thy virtue be
Henceforth against the Syren-voice more strong,

Lay down the cause of tears, and list to me;
And thou shalt hear how in far different guise
Thou shouldst have walk'd when I was hid from thee.

For never Art or Nature to thine eyes
Show'd aught so lovely as the form, wherein
I dwelt, and which in dust and ashes lies

If of the highest gladness thou hast been
Depriv'd by Death, what thing of mortal birth
Should then have had the power thy heart to win

When thou hadst felt how fleeting is the worth
Of things of time, thou shouldst have striven to me,

And follow me, no longer of the earth;

   Nor turn away thy pinion from the skies,

And wait more wounds, or from a maiden's love,

Or other trifle that so quickly dies.

   The fledgeling twice or thrice deceit may prove;

But all in vain the fowler's art is spent

Against the bird that with strong wings doth move."

   As children stand, when chid, with eyelids bent

To earth, and, silent and ashamed, receive

Reproof for that whereof they do repent,

   Thus was I now. She said. " If thou dost grieve

So sore for what thou hearest, raise thou now

Thy beard, and what thou seest more woe shall leave "

   With less resistance is the oak laid low,

Uprooted by the storms from our own land,

Or those which from Iarbas' kingdom blow,

   Than I obey'd, unwilling, her command;

For, in her speech when beard my face she hight,

The venom'd sting I well might understand.

   And when I upwards look'd, there met my sight,

As first they had appear'd, those creatures pure,

Who stay'd them from their shower of blossoms bright,

And then my eyes, although not yet secure,
Saw Beatrice on that strange form, wherein
Two natures in one person aye endure.

Though veiled, and beyond the margin green,
Yet did she now her ancient self excel,
As, then, all other loveliness, I ween.

Thus the sharp thorn of penitence so well
Pierced to my heart, that in each earthly thing
Which most I loved, most bitterness did dwell;

And in my thought it touch'd so deep a spring
Of sorrow, that I fell, as one half dead:
She knows the rest, who did my madness bring.

When life once more around my heart was shed,
The Lady I at first beheld alone,
Near me I saw, and "Hold by me," she said.

Into the flowing stream she me had drawn,
And bearing me along with her, pass'd o'er
The waves, as light as shuttle swiftly thrown.

When I was nigh unto the blessed shore,
"*Asperges me*," so sweetly to mine ear
Came, that my memory writes it now no more.

Then she her arms toward me stretch'd, and here

Plunged me beneath the waves, till o'er my head
The waters flow'd in current swift and clear.

  Thence I, all bathed and purified was led
Unto the dance of the four maidens bright,
Who, with extended arms, to meet me sped.

  "Here, we are nymphs, in heaven, four stars of
      light:
Ere Beatrice went down to earth, were we
Ordain'd to serve as handmaids in her sight.

  We to her eyes will lead thee; but the three,
Whom yonder thou beholdest, will give aid,
That in their depths of splendour thou mayst see."

  Thus they began their song; and then they led
My steps unto the winged steed: and there,
Turn'd unto us, was Beatrice.   They said:

  "To look upon her now thou needst not spare;
Thee have we placed before those emeralds bright,
Whence Love his arrows did, of old, prepare."

  A thousand longings, of more burning might
Than flames of glowing fire, now drew mine eyes
Unto her eyes, whose soft and shining light

  Upon her steed was fix'd.   As sunlight bea

In a clear mirror, so there met my gaze
That creature's doubly strange diversities.

   Reader, thou well mayst think what deep amaze
Fill'd all my mind, when thus the thing I saw,
 Unchanged itself, yet changed within the rays

   Reflecting it.   In gladness and in awe,
My spirit tasted of the heavenly streams,
Which eating, to fresh thirst doth surely draw.

   And then those three, who in their acts did seem
As of the highest hierarchy of Heaven,
Advanced, in measure to the angel hymn.

   They sang : " Now turn thee, Beatrice, and even
Thy holy gaze on this thy servant place ;
For he, to see thee, through sore toil hath striven.

   Of grace, we pray thee, show to us such grace,
Thy brow unveiling, that he may discern
The more than former beauty of thy face."

   O splendour of the living light etern,
Who that hath paled his cheek beneath the shade
Of high Parnassus, or from its full urn

   Hath deeply quaff'd, yet would not be afraid,
Striving to render what thou didst appear,

When, o'er thy cheek, in harmony there play'd
  The sunbeams, as, reveal'd, thou stoodst in daylight 145
    clear !

CANTO XXXII.

Argument.

Mystical vision.

My eyes were fix'd, so eager and intent
The thirst of ten long weary years to sate,
That all my other senses seem'd as spent ;

And those, on this side and on that, were met
By walls which made them care for nought beside,
Her smile so drew them in its ancient net :

When I, perforce, was turn'd unto the side
Where erst I saw those holy maidens three,
Because they said : "Too fix'd thine eyes abide."

As, after gazing at the sun, ye see
But dimly, dazzled by the radiance bright ;
So, in like manner was it now with me.

But when my eyes were in the lower light
More skill'd, (a lower light, I did but say,
Beside the greater splendour,) to the right,

I saw the glorious army turn away,
Until a radiance beam'd upon each brow,
From the seven lamps and from the solar ray.

As soldiers 'neath their shields for safety draw,
And, 'mid the battle, with their banner turn,
Ere yet they wholly can be moved, I saw

Even thus the legions of the heavenly bourne,
Who form'd the vanguard, all pass on, before
The bending of the car I could discern.

Beside the wheels the maidens eyed once more,
And the wing'd courser drew the holy ark,
The while his plumes he all unruffled bore.

She who had led me through the water dark,
And I and Statius, by that wheel pass'd on,
Which, turning, did a smaller orbit mark.

And, as we wended through the forest, (lone,
For sin of her who to the serpent's speech
Gave ear,) they sang, in sweet, melodious tone

An angel hymn. The arrow's flight might reach

Three times as far as we had onward sped,
When Beatrice her chariot stay'd. From each

  I heard a whispering voice, which "Adam!" said
And then they circled round a tree, whose pride
Of verdant leaves and blossoms all had fled;

  Yet spread it forth its crown so high and wide,
That even amid the Indian forests vast,
Its stately stature well had been descried.

  "But thou, O winged steed, art surely blest,
Abstaining from this tree whose fruit is sweet
At first, but after, of most bitter taste."

  Thus round the leafless trunk, with circling feet
They pass'd, and spake; then he of natures twain :
"Here lives the seed of justice, as is meet."

  Now to his chariot-pole he turn'd again,
And dragg'd it to the stem all bare and riven;
And tied thereto he left it. As, full fain,

  The plants of earth, when unto them is given
The sunny splendour, mingled with the rays
Still following the silvery fish of heaven,

  Bud, in the shining of the soft spring days,
And, as of old, each colour o'er them glows,

Ere yet the sun has gone in other ways ;

   More bright than violet, more pale than rose,

Were the new blossoms which the plant did gain,

Where erst had been but dry and wither'd boughs.

   Sooth, to the knowledge of that sweetest strain

Which now they sang, a hymn unheard below,

My weak and weary sense might not attain :

   But, could I track the steps of sleep, and show

How, at the tale of Syrinx, slumber fell

Upon those eyes whose watching work'd their woe,

   As painter doth on his ensample dwell,

I should depict how closed my drowsy eyes ;

But then I needs were skill'd to picture well.

   Thus I pass on, to tell thee in what guise

A splendour rent the veil of sleep from me,

And a voice said : " What dost thou here ?   Arise ! "

   As, to behold the blossoms of that tree,

Whose fruit the holy angels aye hath fed,

In heavenly feast which evermore shall be,

   Peter, and James, and John, of yore were led,

And from their trance were waken'd by the call

At which more heavy slumber once had fled,

And saw their company diminish'd all;

For Moses and Elias both were gone,   80

And even their Lord was clad in changed stole:

   Thus turn'd I; and beheld the dame alone,

Standing anear me, who my steps did aid,

When through the flowing river I was drawn.

   And " Where is Beatrice ?" in doubt I said;   85

And she to me: " Behold her where along

The turf there lies yon tree's new leafy shade.

   Behold the company who round her throng;

Following the wingéd steed the others soar,

With yet a deeper, sweeter voice of song."   90

   I heard not rightly if her words were more,

Because before my longing eyes was that

Which from my mind shut out all other lore.

   Alone upon the holy ground who sat,

As guardian of the car which there was tied   95

By him in whom two natures are innate.

   The seven fair nymphs all hand in hand allied,

Encircled her, and those bright lamps they held,

Which safe from Aquila and Auster 'bide.

   " When thou, a stranger here, shalt have fulfill'd   100

Thy time, thou ever in that Rome with me,
Shalt dwell, where Christ the Roman power doth wield.

   Yet (for the sake of those who evilly
Do walk on earth) when thou hast there return'd,
Look that thou write the things thou here dost see :"

   Thus Beatrice to me.   And I, who burn'd
Her bidding to fulfil, with mind devout,
My eyes and thoughts even as she bade me turn'd.

   Never from out thick clouds the fire is brought
So swiftly, when the summer tempests rove,
Bursting in rain from regions most remote,

   As here I now beheld the bird of Jove
Swoop on the tree ; and branch and stem he broke,
And scatter'd leaves and blossoms through the grove,

   And struck the chariot with so rude a stroke,
It bent, as doth a ship in stormy flood,
Now here, now there, sway'd by the billows' shook.

   And then, in the triumphal car there stood
A fox, whose gaunt and meagre form did show
How fierce his appetite for every food.

   But, smiting him with many an angry blow,
My fairest Lady turn'd him soon to flight

As swift as bones withouten flesh may go :

  And then return'd once more within my sight
The eagle, and full swiftly cleft the air,
And fill'd the chariot with his plumage bright.

  As from a heart that doth some sorrow wear,
A voice came forth from heaven, and thus it spake '
" My ship, thou dost an evil burden bear ! "

  And now it seem'd as from the earth there brake
A dragon, which between the wheels did spring,
And with sharp-pointed tail the chariot strake ;

  Then, as a wasp that pulls away her sting,
Unto himself he drew the dart malign,
And of the car therewith a part did bring,

  And joyful fled in windings serpentine.—
As seed in fertile soil, the plumage, shed
Perchance with meaning holy and benign,

  Now thickly over all the chariot spread,
And hid the whole, within so short a space,
That longer were it ere a sigh had sped

  From open lips.   The holy edifice,
Transform'd thus, now divers heads put forth,
One at each side, three at the foremost place.

The first were like to oxen of this earth,
The rest had but one horn upon their front :
Such creatures strange were ne'er of mortal birth.

　Securely, as a rock on lofty mount,
Seated thereon a harlot I descried,
Who look'd around with gaze of shameless wont.

　And, as in fear to lose her, by her side
A fierce and giant lover did I see ;
And kisses they exchanged.　But she, with wide

　And roving eye, oft turn'd her glance on me ;
Thus I her wrathful paramour beheld
Scourge her full sore, in savage jealousy.

　Then he, with anger and suspicion fill'd,
Loosed from the tree that monstrous form, and fled
Far mid the wood, which o'er me, as a shield

　From those dark Forms of Evil, its bright verdure
　　spread.

CANTO XXXIII.

Argument.

Allegorical predictions. Dante drinks the water of the river
Eunœ, and feels himself worthy to ascend to Heaven

"*Deus venerunt gentes*," in sweet hymn,
Of voice alternating, now three, now four,
The damsels 'gan to chaunt, with weeping dim;
   And Beatrice gave ear unto their lore,
With mien that bore well nigh as sad a trace   5
As Mary's at the cross. And when no more
   The maidens sang, but unto her gave place,
Rising to her full height of majesty
She spake, a burning flush upon her face:
   "A little while, and me ye shall not see,   10
And, sisters dear, a little while again,
And ye shall see me." Now the seven did she

Lead on, and only by a sign she then .
Bade me to follow her, with the fair dame,
And with the ancient Sage who did remain.

Thus pass'd we on ; nor do I think we came
More than ten paces further, when her eyes
Mine eyes transpierced. Then spake she with the same

Calm aspect : " Come more quickly, in such wise
That when it chance I hold discourse with thee,
Thou mayst, unlet by space that 'twixt us lies,

Give ear." Thus pass'd I on full speedily.
She spake : " My brother, wherefore dost not dare
To ask me somewhat, as thou go'st with me ! "

And, as with those who too much reverence wear,
Speaking before the great ones of the earth,
And thence their accents die upon the air,

Even thus with me the words but half came forth,
As I began : " Lady, full well, meseems,
Thou know'st my needs, and that of greatest worth

To aid them." Then she said : " By the false gleams
Of fear and shame no longer walk ; nor speak
In accents like unto a man who dreams.

Know, that the vessel which the serpent brake

Was, and is not ; but be the guilty sure
That God's revenge doth tarry not, for sake

Of funeral sop.   Nor without heir shall 'dure,
For aye, the bird whose plumage made the car
A monster first and afterwards a lure.

For well I see, in each propitious star,
That swift and surely shall the time arrive,
Secure from every let and every bar,

When one, who is five hundred, ten, and five,
Shall, sent by God, the harlot slay, and him
Whose guilt doth from the selfsame source derive.

It well may be that my narration, dim
As Themis or the Sphinx, persuade thee less,
Since it, like them, is shadowy as a dream ;

But soon events shall be the Naïades,
To strip this riddle of its vale of gloom ;
Nor hurt the herbs, nor cause the flocks distress.

Thou note thou well ; and as these words do come
From me, so teach them unto those who live
A life which is a race unto the tomb.

And when thou dost on earth this history give,
See that thou hide not how thou saw'st the tree,

The which two several times despoil'd did grieve.

Know, he who robs its fruit and flowers, and he
Who shatters it, do blaspheme God, who made
It only for his use, in sanctity.

For this, the first-born soul of man was stay'd
Five thousand years and more, in weary pain,
Awaiting him on whom the guilt was laid.

Deep slumber surely must have lull'd thy brain,
If thou dost see not that its changed boughs,
And height, from some strange thing their cause have
      ta'en.

But thy vain thoughts, like Elsa's stream, which flows
In petrifying waves, have dull'd thy mind,
And earthly joys have been as Pyramus

To the white mulberry : else shouldst thou find
Only God's justice in the interdict,
When thou each circumstance hast here combined

But, since I see that in thine intellect
Is the hard substance and the bur of stone,
I bid thee in some feeble sort depict

(Though dazzled by the light that o'er thee shone)
This my discourse : as pilgrims do retain

The palm that in the Holy Land hath grown."

And I : " As wax whereon the seal hath lain,
And from the impress given doth change no more,
Thy words have left their print upon my brain.

But why above my mortal sight dost soar
To such high regions, in thy much-loved speech,
That most I lose when most I seek thy lore ?"

She answer'd me : " Because I thee would teach
To know the school wherein thou erst didst learn,
And if its doctrine to my words can reach ·

And thence thine ancient way thou mayst discern,
How far it lieth from the path divine ;
As far as Earth from highest heavenly bourne"

Wherefore I said : "No memory is mine,
That I did e'er depart from love of thee,
Nor doth my conscience bear an evil sign."

"If in thy heart no memory there be,"
She smiling answer'd, " yet bethink thee now,
That thou hast drunk of Lethe. When ye see

The smoke, then deem ye of the fiery glow ;
Thus, thou in thy forgetfulness mayst seek
And find the proof of all thy guilt and woe.

But henceforth clearly unto thee I speak,
In words whose plainness shall be of more worth
To show the truth unto thy vision weak."

More slow and with more splendour now went forth,
The sun, in crossing the meridian-way,
Which changes in each region of the earth,

When, at the ending of the forest gray,
(Like those whose pale green leaves and mourning
        boughs,
'Neath the dim shining of the northern ray,

Clothe the cold Alpine slopes anear the snows,)
The seven fair maidens stopp'd, as those whose art
Is to lead on a troop, and somewhat shows

Danger at hand.   Here, from a fountain's heart,
Meseem'd both Tigris and Euphrates burst ;
And then, as friends, reluctantly they part.

" Thou, of the human race the brightness, first
In glory, say, what stream its wave doth shed
Thus from our source, so widely then dispersed ?"

And in response unto this prayer was said :
" Of this ask thou Matilda."   She replied,   •
As one on whom some causeless blame is laid :

"This, and all other things thereto allied,
Already have I told him ; and, I ween,
My words have not been hid in Lethe's tide."

And Beatrice : "Within his mind hath been,
Perchance, some greater care ; which oft hath power
To cause the lesser to be dimly seen.

But now thou standest on Eunoe's shore ;
Lead thou him there, as is thy wonted use,
And wake his ancient memory once more."

As gentle spirits make no vain excuse,
But all their will unto another's bend,
Soon as a sign that bidding doth disclose,

Thus she, delaying not, now took my hand,
And unto Statius said, in accents low :
"Thou too come with him to the river-strand."

Reader, had I more space, my song should show,
In part, the sweetness of the crystal stream,
Wherein ye ne'er satiety may know.

But every page is fill'd, which here I deem
Ordain'd unto this second canticle ;
Thus more, in sooth, my art would ill beseem.

Now I came forth from the most holy rill,

Anew created, (as the plants which are

Clothed with fresh leaves in early spring-time still,)

  Pure and disposed aright to rise unto each star.

NOTES.

CANTO I.

V. 7.—"Here let my Lay from Death once more arise,"

Different meanings have been ascribed to this passage; some commentators supposing that "la morta poesia" means the whole poem concerning the three kingdoms of the Dead, and taking "resurga" in the sense of rise higher. Were it so, the translation ought to stand thus

"But higher let the Lay of Death arise."

Resurgere, however, does not mean to rise higher, but to rise again. I have therefore preferred the interpretation of those who suppose "la morta poesin" to mean the strain which sings of the second Death and the abode of everlasting woe. Thus it has here a twofold signification, viz. the poetry which sings of Death, and the poetry which is deathlike and mournful. The revival of poetry in the fourteenth century may also be alluded to.

V 11, 12 —"The selfsame malady which erst they knew
Who mourn, as chattering jays, their hapeless wrong"

The daughters of Pierus, they challenged the Muses to a

trial of skill is made, and, for this presumption, were changed
into chattering, songless birds.

V. 19 —" *The beauteous planet, counsellor of love,*"

The star of Venus.

V 21 — " *Hiding the Fish, that in her escort move.*"

The sun being in Aries, Pisces must necessarily rise before
dawn, and consequently be dimmed by the brighter rays of the
morning star.

V. 21-24 —" *To the right hand I turn'd, and gazed awhile*
At the far pole, and saw four stars, unseen
By man, save on our Parents did beguile"

The four stars are supposed to symbolize the four Cardinal
Virtues; i e prudence, justice, fortitude, and temperance but
there is also an evident allusion to the Southern Cross, Dante's
accurate knowledge of the position of which has excited some
surprise But though it was not till nearly a century later that
Amerigo Vespucci first observed the starry cross in the southern
sky, yet this constellation must have been well known to the
ancient world The Southern Cross is, I believe, visible in
Egypt, Arabia, and Palestine, as well as in more distant lands;
and Dante may have acquired his information either from the
writings of the ancient astronomers, or from the narratives of
more recent travellers It is possible that he was acquainted
with Marco Polo, who, having visited Java and Madagascar,
returned to Venice in 1295 Another circumstance may have
originally suggested this idea to Dante In our northern hemisphere, there are four beautiful stars, which form a Greek Cross
One is Alpheratz, on the forehead of Andromeda; the others are
those Alpergo, Markab, and Algenib, all in Pegasus. In

England, either from the difference of latitude, or the haziness of the atmosphere, these stars might easily remain unnoticed, save by the astronomical student. But, at Sorrento or Capri, the most careless observer cannot fail to be struck with the splendour of that glittering cross there, one's eye always turns to it, and it seems to dim every other constellation It is probable that Dante, when ambassador at Naples, studied astronomy, as he did all other sciences to which he had access , and, indeed, throughout the Purgatorio, we find many traces of his sojourn by the Tyrrhene sea.

V. 29 —" *There where the Wain but now had pass'd away;*"

The Antipodes of Jerusalem is the spot where Dante has placed Purgatory ; consequently, Charles's Wain cannot be seen from the latter place He says

"*the Wain but now had pass'd away,*"

because he and Virgil had but newly arrived in the Antipodes

V. 31.—"*I saw anear me an old man alone ;*"

Cato, surnamed Uticensis, from his death at Utica. It may seem strange that Dante should have placed a heathen and a suicide as guardian of Purgatory , but Cato is here the symbol of the soul set free from the body

V. 61 —" *As I have said, a Lady from on high*"

Beatrice, who descended into Hades, in order to send Virgil to Dante's assistance. (See Inferno, c xi , v 70)

V. 73, 74 —"*And thou must know it well, who hadst no fear Of death, in Utica,*"

Cato stabbed himself at Utica, in Africa, rather than submit to Cæsar   Virgil therefore appeals to him, in behalf of Dante, journeying to seek freedom from the tyranny of sin.

V. 79 —*"Where she who was on earth thy loving wife"*

Marcia, whom Dante has already seen in Hades, among the Shades of the great and good Heathen.

V. 82 —*"Let us throughout thy sevenfold kingdom go;"*

The seven circles of Purgatory.

V. 95.—*"And gird this wand'rer with the reeds that rise"*

The reeds are supposed to be the emblems of simplicity, lowliness, and docility; the dew probably signifies penitence.

V. 98 —*"The angel-ministrant of Paradise"*

The angelic guardian of the gate of Purgatory.

V. 113, 114.—*"Let us turn back, for thou may, it must be,*
The plain descends unto the waves below."

Showing that the penitent must abase himself ere he can ascend

V. 130-132.—*"Now we were come unto the desert shore*
Of that great sea, upon whose waters wide
He who hath sail'd returns again no more"

In the original,

> *"Venimmo poi in sul lito diserto,*
> *Che mai non vide navicar sua acque*
> *Uom, che di ritornar sia poscia esperto."*

Shakspere's,

> *"undiscover'd country, from whose bourne*
> *No traveller returns,"*

is a curious coincidence of thought   it can scarcely be imitation.

CANTO II.

V. 1, 2.—"*The sun now low on the horizon lay,*
On the horizon of the Holy Land,"

As Dante supposes the mountain of Purgatory to be the Antipodes of Jerusalem, the sun was, of course, setting on Mount Sion, when rising in Purgatory.

V. 4, 5.—"*And night, who aye opposed to him doth stand,*
Came slowly forth from out the Ganges stream."

Night seems to come from the east, as the sun sinks in the west.

V. 6 —"*Bearing the Balance.*"

The sign of Libra.

V. 27.—"*Borne by those wings of white and glittering hue.*"

Here again we find traces of Dante's residence in Naples. No one can see the Neapolitan boats, with their lateen sails, without perceiving the resemblance to a white-winged bird.

V. 55-57.—"*The sun was shooting down the burning day,*
The fiery darts with which his skilful bow
From half the sky had chased the Goat away"

Capricorn is ninety degrees, or a quarter of the sphere, distant from Aries, in which the sun was, at the date of Dante's visit to Purgatory. Thus, as far as Capricorn had passed the meridian, so far must the sun here rise above the horizon.

V. 70.—"*And, as to him who wears an olive wreath,*"

Matilda of peace worn wreaths of olive in the days of Dante.

V. 91.—"*I said 'My own Casella,'*"

Casella was a Florentine musician of great talent, and a friend of Dante. Crescimbini, in his *Storia della Volgar Poesia*, says that he found in the Vatican a song or madrigal, set to music by Casella, and written by Lemmo of Pistoia, who flourished towards the end of the thirteenth century. The title page of this composition is this—*Lemmo da Pistoja, e Casella diede il suono.* He seems also to have set Dante's songs to music.

V. 92, 93 ——"*but why so long*
Hast thou delay'd to reach thy journey's scope?"

There are different opinions regarding this passage. The simple explanation seems to be, that Dante supposes the souls of the dead to roam among the dreary marshes at the mouth of the Tiber, before they are admitted to purge away their sin in Purgatory. This idea is partly borrowed from the ancients, who believed that the Shades wandered on the banks of the Styx, stretching out their hands longingly to the farther shore, before the bark of Charon received them. Certainly no spot could be chosen, more fit for a restless, homeless spirit than that most desolate land at the mouth of the Tiber. Some commentators, however (the great name of Lombardi among the number), instead of supposing that Casella had been dead for some time, imagine that he had died on board a vessel sailing down the Tiber, on his return from the Jubilee; and thus they sweep away the whole myth regarding the wanderings of the dead in the Latian Maremma. But, although in most cases it is safe to trust to Lombardi, yet here there are difficulties in the way. Casella, being an intimate friend of Dante, was probably about the same age, namely, thirty-five, at the time of the Jubilee. Why, then, should Dante express surprise at his delay? He more naturally would have asked him how he had been cut off so early. Lombardi, on the other hand, argues that the appointed place for those who had delayed repentance was the *anti purgatorio*, and, to get over some difficulties, reads *terra* for *era*, which former is indeed the reading of no fewer than ninety manuscripts, including many of the highest authority, and, among others, that attributed to Boccaccio, in the Vatican. The Accademia della Crusca, however, has decided that the word should be *era*, not *terra*; and its reading has the incontestable advantage of making sense, which the other does not. But, in the absence of any precise information respecting the death of Casella, the point must remain uncertain.

V. 98, 91. ———" Three months have fled
   Since all who would may freely enter here."

That is, during the Jubilee of 1300.

V. 112 —" Love, that within my heart discourseth still,"
   " Amor, che nella mente mi ragiona."

This is the first line of a song written by Dante, and set to music by Casella.

CANTO III.

V. 20 —"*For I perceived no shadow by my side.*"

In hell, as there was no sun, there was no shadow; thus Dante is here, for the first time, made aware of the difference between his own mortal body and the airy, unsubstantial shades.

V. 25, 26.—"*In Naples now, beneath the vesper-star,*
My body lies."

Virgil died B. C. 19, at Brundusium, now Brindisi, whither he had gone to meet Augustus, then returning from the East. By his own desire his body was conveyed to Naples, and buried beside the highroad leading to Puteoli and Cumæ, and there his tomb remains to this day. During the Middle Ages this sepulchre was venerated almost as a shrine. Sundry Italians made a pilgrimage to Naples, for the sole purpose of visiting this spot: here Petrarch planted a laurel; and here Boccaccio resolved to be no longer a merchant, but a man of letters.

V. 29, 30 —"*Thou shouldst not marvel more than at the skies,*
Because on them the sunbeams are not stay'd."

In Dante's time it was believed that the heavens were transparent hollow spheres, one within the other.

V. 41, 42.—"*Some, whose sore longing for the good they seek*
Is given to them as grief, for evermore."

The unbaptised in Hades. (See Inferno, Canto IV.)

V. 46 — "*Between Turbia and Lerici's bound.*"

Lerici, near Spezia, and Turbia, above Monaco. The space between them includes the whole Riviera, or Corniche road; which, till within the last fifty years, was precipitous and full of dangers.

V. 112 — "*Know, I am Manfred, of imperial race.*"

Manfred, first Regent, then King of Naples, natural son of the emperor Frederick II , and champion of the Ghibelline cause. He was defeated by Charles of Anjou, brother of St Louis, at the battle of Benevento, Feb 26th, 1266, and there he lost both crown and life ; thus Dante, who was born in 1265, could not have seen him on earth

When Charles first entered the kingdom, Manfred endeavoured to enter into negotiations with him, but received the following message in quaint old French "*Alles et dit mon à le Sultan de Loetre, e je metrai lui en enfers, e il metra moi en paradis.*"

Manfred was one of the most gifted and chivalrous princes of the Middle Ages He seems to have been the idol of his people, and even his Saracen subjects were devoted to him He appears, indeed, to have possessed a peculiar power of winning affection, if we may judge by the passionate grief his followers showed at his death. Even grave historians linger lovingly over the details of his person and character, such as his love of wearing the colour green, his fair and noble aspect, and his delight in the society of poets and troubadours.

V. 115, 116 — "*Unto my daughter go to her of whom
Are sprung the kings of Sicily and Spain*"

Manfred's daughter Constance married Peter, King of

Arragon, who occupied Sicily after the famous Sicilian
Vespers, in 1282. She was mother of Frederick, King of
Sicily, and James, King of Arragon.

V. 124, 125.—"*And if Cosenza's pastor, sent in charge
Of me by Clement.*"

Bartolommeo Pignatelli, Archbishop of Cosenza, sent by
Clement IV., to incite Charles against Manfred.

V. 125.—"*How of the mind of God to read this face.*"
In the original,
"*Avesse in Dio ben letto questa faccia.*"

Faccia here meaning either the facet of a precious stone, or
the side of an engraved gem; and thus signifying the many
sidedness, the manifold wisdom and goodness of God.

V. 129.—"*Well guarded by the heavy pile of stones.*"

Manfred was buried, in the first instance, at the bridge
of Benevento, and the soldiers each threw a stone on his
grave, to serve as a monument. The body was afterwards
disinterred, by order of the Archbishop of Cosenza, and
carried beyond the kingdom of Naples, to the banks of the
river Verde. This was done because the Archbishop had
sworn to chase Manfred from the realm. Dante here calls
the kingdom of Naples simply "*il Regno*," as the inhabitants
of the border countries of the Neapolitan and Roman states do
to this day.

V. 132.—"*Whence from the realm 'twas borne with torches spent.*"

The extinguished lights are a sign of excommunication

CANTO IV.

V. 5, 6.—"*And thus disproves the error that believes*
 Soul above soul our nature doth contain."

Alluding to the Platonists, who believed that man had three souls: the vegetative, in the liver; the sensitive, in the heart; and the intellectual in the brain.

V. 25, 26.—"*The foot of man to Noli may go down,*
 And climb St. Leo, and Bismantua's height."

St. Leo, a town in the duchy of Urbino, curiously perched on a high and apparently inaccessible rock. Noli, a city and castle, backed by high mountains on the Riviera of Genoa. Bismantua, said to be a high mountain in Modena; but it is not marked on the maps, and none of the commentators seem able to describe exactly its position.

V. 56, 57.—"*Up to the sun I gazed, and saw that earth*
 From the left side was stricken by its flame."

As Dante sat with his face to the east, the sun of course struck his left side, Purgatory being in the southern hemisphere.

V. 61, 62.   —— "*If the Twin Brethren, bright*
 Castor and Pollux, near yon mirror lay."

That is, if the Sun were in Gemini, instead of in Aries.

V. 70, 71.   ———" the road
Where Phaeton his chariot drove so ill "

That is, the path of the Sun   Phaeton, son of Apollo and
Clymene, begged of his father to allow him to drive the chariot
of the Sun for one day   Apollo, having previously sworn by
the Styx to grant whatever he asked, could not draw back,
and accordingly instructed him how to drive so as to do as little
mischief as possible.   These directions not being attended to,
the heavens were soon on fire.   Jupiter, to save the world from
destruction, smote Phaeton with a thunderbolt, and he fell
dead into the river Po, where he still seems to be mourned by
his sisters, the Heliades, transformed, according to the legend,
into the tall poplars, which to this day stand sadly on the
banks of the stream

V. 105.—" Some, who appear'd, in sooth, a listless band."

Those who, from indolence, have delayed repentance till near
their death

V. 106 —" And one who seem'd with weariness down-weigh'd."

Belacqua, an excellent maker of musical instruments, but
remarkable for his indolence

V. 123, 124   ———" Belacqua, for thy plight
I grieve no more."

Dante seems to have feared that Belacqua had died impenitent.

V. 187-189 ————"for o'er
Our heads is shining now the noonday sun,
And dusky twilight stealeth toward Morocco's
shore."

According to Dante's system, it was evening on the coast of Morocco, at noon in Purgatory.

CANTO V.

V. 27.—"And changed their song to a long, startled 'Oh!'"

In the original,

" Mutar lo canto in un O lungo e roco "

V. 64 —"And one began," &c.

The speaker is Jacopo del Cassero, a noble of Fano, who, being at enmity with Azzolino III. of Este, was assassinated by his orders at Oriaco, near Padua, among the lagunes.

V. 68, 69. ————"when the land thou dost behold
That lies 'twixt Naples and Romagnan ground."

The March of Ancona.

V. 74 —"The blood where I abode "

Alluding to the doctrine of Empedocles, who believed that the soul dwelt in the blood.

V. 75.—"Within Antenor's land."

Antenor, a Trojan prince, related to Priam. It is said that, during the siege of Troy, he corresponded secretly with the Greeks, and especially with Menelaus and Ulysses. In the council of Priam, Homer represents him advising the Trojans to restore Helen, and thereby conclude the war. He encouraged the Greeks to make the wooden horse, which, at his persuasion, was brought into the city by a breach made in the walls. After the destruction of Troy, Antenor went to Italy, and founded Padua, which was therefore called the city of Antenor.

V. 79.—"But had I taken my flight by Mira's path."

La Mira, a small place on a canal near Padua.

V. 85.—"Then said another."

This other is Buonconte, son of Count Guido di Montefeltro. He was killed June 11th, 1289, at Certomondo, in the plain of Campaldino, in the Casentino. Buonconte, on this occasion, commanded the Ghibelline forces, and Dante fought among the Guelphs. The Florentines dedicated a church to St. Barnabas, in commemoration of the victory won by the Guelphs on the day dedicated to that saint.

V. 92.—"That of thy sepulchre man knoweth not."

The body of Buonconte was never found, so this narrative is purely imaginary.

V. 96.—"Above the convent born, in Apennine."

The Convent of the Camaldoli, founded about A.D. 1009 by St. Romualdo. Some of the pines failed there lately, for the building of St. Paul's at Rome, were believed to be four centuries old.

V. 97.—"There where its early name becometh vain."

Where the Archiano loses itself in the Arno.

V. 117.—"From Pratomagno to the furthest height."

Pratomagno divides the Val d'Arno, properly so called, from the Casentino, or upper valley.

V. 133.—"Then spake a third."

This third speaker is Pia Tolomei, whom Dante here places among those who have met with a violent death. But the common opinion is, that she was not actually murdered by her jealous husband, but sent to his castle in the Maremma, and there allowed to die of marsh-fever.

V. 134.—"Who me, already undone'd, took to be his bride."

The maiden name of Pia Tolomei was Guastelloni. She first married one of the Tolomei family, of Sienna; and, being left a widow, she then married Pagnello Pannocchieschi, lord of Castel della Pietra, who, either from unfounded jealousy, or from a wish to get rid of her, imprisoned her in his castle in the pestilential Maremma, where, if he did not actually cause her to be murdered, the climate soon did its deadly work.

CANTO VI.

V. 13 —"*There did the Aretine onward press.*"

The Aretine was a certain Messer Benincasa of Arezzo, who, when he was deputy of the Podestà, or governor of Sienna, put to death Taoco, brother of Ghino di Taoco, of Amalunga, for the crime of brigandage. Ghino, to revenge the death of his brother, came to Rome, where Benincasa was auditor of the Rota, and entering suddenly the room where the tribunal was sitting, kill'd him, and cutting off his head, carried it with him, and made his escape from the city. This Ghino, after being long the terror of the Siennese Maremma, and of the Court of Rome itself, made peace with Boniface VIII, who presented him with a rich benefice, and created him a senator! His stronghold was at Radicofani, where he established a system of brigandage not wholly eradicated at this day.

V. 16.—"*And he who drown'd, in running from the chase.*"

This was a youth named Guccio de' Tarlati, of Arezzo, who, being hotly pursued after the defeat of Bibiena, fell into the Arno, and was drowned.

V. 17, 18.—"*The younger Frederick, and the Pisan knight*
Who show'd the good Marzucco strong in pain."

Frederick, son of Count Guido di Battifolle, was killed by one of the Bostoli family. The Pisan knight, Farinata degli Scoringiani, of Pisa, being killed by Messer Bacone of Caprona, gave occasion to his father, Marzucco, to show both fortitude in bearing sorrow, and meekness in forgiving his enemies. It is related of Marmoce (who had become a Minor Friar) that he exhorted his relations to make peace with him who had killed his son, and not to seek revenge.

V. 18.—"*I saw Count Orso*"

Some commentators believe Count Orso to have been of the Alberti family, and to have been treacherously murdered by some of his own relations. Others say that he was the son of Count Napoleone da Cerbaia, and that he was killed by his uncle, Count Albert da Mangona. The latter seems the more authentic account.

V. 22.—"*Of Peter de la Brosse I speak.*"

Pierre de la Brosse was born of an obscure family in Touraine. He was physician to St. Louis; and, under Philip the Hardy, attained such power, that everything was done according to his counsels. This stirred up envy against him; and his affection for the king's children by his first wife, Isabella of Arragon, excited the hatred of Mary of Brabant, second wife of Philip. But the pretext upon which his ruin was effected is not certainly known. Some say that he had accused the queen of poisoning Louis, her eldest stepson; whereupon the courtiers, filled with envy of the powerful minister, maintained her innocence, and, besides finding him guilty of calumny, further accused him of selling his master's secrets to the Castilians. Others say that the queen accused him of attempts against her virtue. But, whatever may have been the accusation, it is certain that Pierre de la Brosse was tried by a secret tribunal, condemned, and hanged in 1874.

V. 28-30   ———"*It seems thou dost deny,*
      O my Enlightener, somewhere in thy lay,
      That prayers can bend the counsels of the sky."

In the sixth Book of the Æneid, where the Sibyl replies to Palinurus,

   "*Desine fata Deûm flecti sperare precando.*"

     V. 74 — "*I am Sordello,*" &c.

Sordello of Mantua, a man of great learning and wisdom, and a celebrated troubadour, who, though Italian by birth, wrote in the Provençal language. Raymond Berenger, Count of Provence, took him into his service.

    V. 88, 89 — "*What boots it that on that Justinian lays*
      The bridle, if the saddle be not filled ?"

That is, what is the use of good laws, if there is no ruler to put them in execution.

V. 93. — "*If thou wouldst understand what God hath will'd.*"

Dante's theory seems to have been, that there ought to be two rulers on earth; one solely for temporal, the other solely for spiritual matters.

     V. 97. — "*O German Albert.*"

Albert of Austria, Emperor of Germany, son of Rudolph of Hapsburg, always refused to enter Italy.

    V. 107 — "*Monaldi, Filippeschi.*"
   Noble Ghibelline families of Orvieto.

V. 111.—"*And look how safe it is in Santafior!*"

Santafior, an Imperial fief in the Sienese Maremma. In Dante's time, owing to the negligence of the Emperor, it was full of tumults and robberies.

V. 126.—"*With pride, as though Marcellus were each one.*"

It is uncertain to which of the illustrious Romans of this name Dante here refers. But it seems probable that he alludes to that Marcellus who opposed Julius Cæsar.

V. 127.—"*Byzans, my Florence,*" &c.

This passage is bitterly ironical.

CANTO VII.

V. 66.—"*A vale like those of earth.*"

Here those spirits who have delayed repentance in consequence of a too exclusive occupation with the affairs of earth are obliged to wait for admittance into Purgatory.

V. 82, 83.—"*Salve regina, on the flowery green*
The spirits sat and sung."

Salve Regina is the beginning of an antiphon in praise of the Virgin · it is commonly sung in the Roman Catholic churches, at the service of Compline. Poggiali says: "In this antiphon, introduced into the Divine Offices about the time of Dante, the

world is called 'a vale of tears;' then, perhaps for this reason,
he imagines it to be sung in this vale of Purgatory."

V. 91.—"*He who is seated highest in the throng.*"

Rudolph of Hapsburg, founder of the house of Austria. He
was born in 1218, elected Emperor of Germany in 1273, and
died at Spires in 1290

V. 97.—"*He who to give him comfort seemeth fain.*"

Ottocar, king of Bohemia, to whom Rudolph of Hapsburg
was at one time Grand Marshal. It is difficult to imagine
why Dante has represented Ottocar as here trying to comfort
Rudolph, for at the close of their lives they were bitter enemies.
It may be that a lesson on peace and forgiveness is here
intended. ° The facts are as follows After Rudulph was elected
Emperor, he assembled a Diet at Mentz, where the deliberations
turned upon the conduct of certain princes who had protested
against the election of the Count of Hapsburg Among these
was Rudolph's former master, the King of Bohemia, against
whom the Diet had other causes of dissatisfaction He had
seized the Duchy of Austria after the death of Frederick, the
last Duke; and the States complained of the oppressions they
suffered under this usurper, from whom they begged to be
delivered. A second Diet was summoned on this subject at
Augsburg, where Ottocar, not appearing, nor doing homage by
his ambassadors, was declared a rebel against the empire His
possession of Austria, Styria, Carniola, and Carinthia was
adjudged illegal, and the Emperor was desired to divest him of
these territories When this sentence was notified to the king,
he exclaimed ˙ "To whom should I do homage? I owe
Rudolph nothing, he was formerly my servant, and I paid him

his wages. My pretensions I will maintain with the point of my sword." Having formed this resolution, he associated himself with several other German princes, and endeavoured to oppose the Emperor by force. But he was at last obliged to submit, and not only gave up the contested territories, but did homage for Bohemia and Moravia.

This homage was performed in an island of the Danube, under a closed canopy, in order to save the proud Ottocar from a public humiliation. Glittering with gold and jewels, he repaired to the place. Rudolph, prouder still, received him in the most coarse and simple dress; and in the middle of the ceremony, either by accident or design (probably the latter), the curtains fell back, and revealed the haughty king on his knees, with his hands joined between those of his conqueror, who had been his Grand Marshal, and whom he had so often called his servant.

The wife of Ottocar, a Russian princess, no less haughty than her husband, was so enraged at this, that she persuaded him to break the treaty he had made with Rudolph, and again have recourse to arms for the recovery of Austria. The Emperor immediately marched against him, and near Vienna a battle ensued, in which Ottocar was killed (1277).

V. 100, 101. ———" *of greater worth*
From youth, than Wenceslaus his son."

Wenceslaus IV., celebrated for cruelty and tyranny, although he is said to have heard mass twenty times a day.

V. 103 —" *And he who on close counsel seems to be.*"

Philip III., of France, surnamed the Hardy, father of Philip le Bel.

V. 104 — "*With one of gentle aspect.*

With Henry III., King of Navarre, and Count of Champagne. He was father-in-law of Philip le Bel.

V. 105 — "*He died, dishonouring the fleur-de-lis.*"

Philip the Hardy, being at war with Peter III., of Arragon, was defeated in a naval battle by Ruggieri Doria, Admiral of the Arragonese fleet. In consequence, being no longer able to convey provisions to his troops in Catalonia, Philip was obliged to abandon his enterprise and take refuge in Perpignan, where he shortly afterwards died of grief.

V. 107. ——"*the curse of France.*"

Philip le Bel.

V. 112 — "*And he who such a stalwart frame doth show.*"

Peter III., of Arragon, crowned in 1276. He married Constance, daughter of Manfred, and occupied Sicily after the famous Sicilian Vespers.

V. 112. — "*And him of manly features joins in song.*"

This latter is Charles I. of Sicily, commonly called Charles of Anjou. Here also two bitter enemies are joined in peace and forgiveness.

V. 115. — "*If to the youth behind him in the throng.*"

Alfonso, eldest son of Peter III. He succeeded his father, in 1285, and died without children, in 1291, at the early age of twenty-nine.

V. 119, 120.—"*Frederick and Giacopo possess the land,*
　　　　But of the better part have nought retain'd."

Giacopo, or James, succeeded his father on the throne of Arragon, Frederick, on that of Sicily ; but neither of them inherited his virtues and talents.

V. 121-123.—"*Full rarely through the branches doth ascend*
　　　　The worth of human virtue : thus He wills
　　　　Who gives it, that to him all praise may tend."

Because, if talents and virtues were hereditary, men would claim them as their own by right, and not give praise to God.

V. 126.—"*Thus Pugha and Provence have many ills.*"

Evils caused by the misgovernment of the son of Charles of Anjou.

V. 128, 129.—"*As much as Constance boasts more joy as wife,*
　　　　Than Beatrice and Margaret's fate doth bring"

Constance was wife of Peter of Arragon ; Beatrice of Provence was the first, Margaret of Burgundy the second wife of Charles of Anjou. Thus the meaning is, that Charles II. of Naples was as much inferior to his father, Charles of Anjou, as this latter was to Peter of Arragon.

V. 130-132.—"*And there, behold the king of simple life,*
　　　　Henry of England, sitting all alone
　　　　His offshoots more with virtuous deeds are rife."

Henry III. of England, seated all alone, to signify how rare simplicity of life is among kings. Dante calls him more

fortunate in his posterity, because of the talents and prosperous
reign of his son, Edward I.

V. 134.—"*The Marquis William,*" &c.

William, Marquis of Montferrat, here in a lower place,
because not of royal rank. He was taken prisoner by the
citizens of Alessandria della Paglia, and shut up in a cage,
where he died of misery in 1292. A bloody war ensued
between the men of Alessandria and the sons of the Marquis
William, in which the inhabitants of Monferrato and the
Canavese suffered many evils.

CANTO VIII.

V. 1.—"*Now was the hour that hath the softest spell,*" &c.

Byron has closely imitated this passage from Dante.

V. 14.—"*Singing Te lucis ante.*"

The first words of a Compline hymn.

V. 38.—"*Safe from the snake that hither soon will glide.*"

The snake is supposed to be an emblem of the dangers
lurking in earthly power and greatness.

V. 53.—"*Gentle Judge Nino, I rejoiced for thee.*"

Nino, or Giovannino Visconti, of Pisa, Judge of the Giudi-
catura of Gallura, in the island of Sardinia, and chief of the
Guelph party. He was driven from Pisa in 1288, and died

seen afterwards fighting against his fellow citizens. Dante had known him at the siege of Caprona, in 1270, and seems to have feared that he had died impenitent.

V. 71. — *" Bid my Joanna that her prayers arise "*

Joanna, daughter of Nino Visconti, and wife of Riccardo da Caruino, of Treviso.

V. 72. — *" I think her mother loves me now no more."*

Beatrice Marchesotti, wife of Nino, and afterwards of Galeazzo Visconti of Milan. This second marriage took place in 1300. Beatrice was then thirty-two, and Galeazzo only twenty-nine.

V. 79-81 — *" For her, in sooth, Gallura's bird had made*
A statelier show about her sepulchre,
Than Milan's snake which shall be o'er her laid."

The cock was the coat of arms of Gallura; that of the Visconti of Milan was the well known snake, still sculptured on the ruins of the old castle of the Visconti at Monza.

V. 89. — *" At those three stars I gaze."*

Many conjectures have been hazarded respecting the three stars here mentioned; but it seems most probable that the constellation of the Triangle is meant. The only difficulty is, that, being near the Southern Cross, the Triangle could not be seen at sunset in the same position as the Cross at dawn. But Dante may either have received imperfect information, or, as he was not writing a treatise on astronomy, may have altered the actual position to suit his narrative. Symbolically, those three stars here signify Faith, Hope, and Charity. These, being the contemplative virtues, are seen in the evening; whereas the four active virtues, Justice, Temperance, Fortitude, and Prudence, are seen in the morning.

V. 114.—" *Till Valdimagra or its boundary came.*"

The valley of the Magra, in the principality of Massa di Carrara, governed, in Dante's time, by the Malaspina.

V. 118.—"*For Conrad Malaspina was my name.*"

There are some doubts as to which of the Malaspinas here speaks. But the most common opinion is, that this Conrad was the father of Moroello Malaspina, who afterwards received Dante so hospitably in his territory of the Lunigiana.

It was when residing with the Malaspinas that Dante first began in earnest to write the Divine Comedy. Many years before, in his first sorrow at the death of Beatrice, he had resolved to write of her "that which had never yet been written of any woman," and well did he keep his vow. But, in his day, the *Vulgar Poesy*, as it was termed, was considered to be a trivial thing, only fit for love sonnets and songs. So he began his great work in Latin, and finished seven cantos. Then came the toils of active life, offices of state, embassies to Rome and Naples; during which, however, he stored up many a curious fact, many a lovely image, all to re-appear in his poem. Next came the troubles of Florence, and at last, exile. And the seven cantos were left, forgotten, in an old chest of drawers. Some years after, his wife, Gemma Donati, found the manuscript, and sent it to the Lunigiana, where Dante had taken refuge. Being counselled by Moroello Malaspina to go on with the poem, he attempted to do so in Latin, but was soon convinced, to use his own words, "that many things which he wicked to say, could not be said save in rhyme." He accordingly began it once more, in vulgar rhymes, as it was then called.

Probably the happiest time of the poet's long exile was passed under the hospitable roof of the Malaspinas.

— — — —

CANTO IX

V. 1.—" *Now Tithon's mistress, famed in ancient song* "

Aurora, of whom Tithon begged immortality This was granted, but as he had forgotten to ask also for perpetual youth, he soon grew old, infirm, and decrepit, and life being unsupportable, he entreated Aurora to withdraw her fatal gift Accordingly, as he could not die, she changed him into a grass-hopper

V. 8.—" *In figure of the creature swift and cold* "

Some ancient commentators believe this to be the sign of the Scorpion, in which case the " silver light " must here be the lunar aurora.   Others say that " the creature swift and cold " was the sign of Pisces, and the whitening of the eastern sky the morning dawn The former, though less commonly received, appears to me the more probable opinion Dante does not give us any reason to believe that he passed the whole night in conversation with the Shades in the Valley of Princes, and it seems natural that he should go to sleep at moonrise, and awoke at sunrise. Besides, the description altogether agrees better with moonlight than with the dawn of day, and the creature that strikes with its tail to more like a scorpion than a fish. Lastly, Dante says, a little farther on, that the third hour of night was just past; and according to the astronomical tables cited by Lombardi, the moon must have risen, preceded by Scorpio, three hours after sunset, on the 7th April, 1300, that being the date of Dante's visit to the Valley of Princes.

V. 18.—"*And in their vision almost are divine.*"
Alluding to the old belief in the truth of morning dreams.

V. 54 —"*I am Lucia.*"
Lucia, symbolically, Divine Light. (See Inferno, Canto II. v. 97.)

V. 94, 95 ————"*the first was a bright mass
Of snowy marble, polish'd clear and pure.*"
The symbol of sincerity

V. 97.—"*The second was of dusky hue obscure,*" &c.
The symbol of contrition.

V. 100-102 —"*The last lay heavy on the former twain,
And seem'd to me of porphyry as bright
As blood that gushes forth from out a vein.*"
The symbol of the love of God

V. 112, 113,—"*He, with his sword, seven times upon my brow
Wrote the first letter of the plague of sin.*"
The angel wrote seven times, on Dante's forehead, the letter P, being the initial of the Italian word peccato, or sin.

V. 115 —*" His garments were of ashen hue, I ween."*

Indicating humility and penitence.

CANTO X.

V. 15 — *" The darken'd border of the moon was low."*

Thus being the fifth day after the moon was full, it must have set nearly four hours after sunrise. Thus, as the sun had been up two hours when Dante awoke, he must have been two hours climbing the steep ascent.

V. 32 —*" So fair, they Polycletus put to shame "*

Polycletus, a celebrated sculptor of Sicyon, about 223 years before the Christian era. He was universally considered the most skilful artist among the ancients, while only the second place was given to Phidias.

V. 74, 75. — *" Of him who caused St. Gregory to seek*
The vict'ry that the gate of Hell unroll'd."

According to the legend, Pope Gregory the Great, when reading the history of Trajan, was so moved by the consideration of his good and great qualities, that he prayed to God for his salvation. But an angel replied to St. Gregory · " The justice of God must be satisfied. Who will bear his penance in the world ?" Then St. Gregory took it all upon himself, and from that day was troubled with many grievous pains and infirmities, which he bore to the end of his life, in order to free the soul of Trajan from hell.   St. Thomas Aquinas has recorded his literal belief in this legend.

CANTO XI.

V. 58, 59 —"*I was of Latium; and my Tuscan sire,*
                      Guglielmo Aldobrandeschi."

He who now speaks is Humbert, son of Guglielmo Aldo-brandeschi, of the family of the Counts of Santafiore.   He was killed at Campagnatico, in the Maremma, by the Siennese, who detested him for his pride.   Dante frequently uses *Latin* and *Latium* for Italy in general, and especially for the province of the Maremma.

V. 74 —"*And one (not he who spoke) then call'd to me.*"

This is Oderisi of Gubbio, an excellent animal-painter, of the school of Cimabue.   He died a little before 1300. Boniface VIII. employed him in Rome to illuminate books along with Giotto.

V. 80, 81 —"*The honour of Agubbio, and that art*
                       In Paris called illumining?"

The art of illuminating manuscripts, though not invented in France, first received its name there.

V. 82 —"*Nay, Francis of Bologna did import,*" &c.

Franco Bolognese, a still more excellent artist than Oderisi. Malvasia, in his *Felsina pittrice*, says that from this Franco, Bologna received the first seeds of the art of painting.

V. 95, 96. ———"Giotto now
Doth cause the former fame to be obscure."

When Giotto was painting the Scrovigni Chapel at Padua, Dante lodged with him, and frequently accompanied him to his work, assisting him with his advice in the composition of those exquisite frescoes. Among his other talents, Dante was an excellent draughtsman.

V. 97, 98 —"Thus from one Guido doth the glory go
Unto another, of the gift of song."

Guido Cavalcanti, Dante's greatest friend, eclipsed the fame of Guido Guinicelli of Bologna, whose poems are of an earlier date. Cavalcanti died in 1301, Guinicelli in 1276.

V. 99, 100.—"And he perchance is born, who will bring low
The pride of both."

It is believed that Dante here predicts his own surpassing greatness. Whether intentional or not, the prophecy has been fulfilled.

V. 111.—"Of him who painfully the path doth try."

Provenzano Salvani, in his day a noted leader of the Ghibelline party, valiant in war, and skilful in peace, but proud and presumptuous. He defeated the Florentines at the battle of the Arbia, but was afterwards defeated and killed by Cambertaio, leader of the Guelphs, near Colle, in Valdelsa (1269).

V. 133.—"Begging for alms, he humbly did entreat"

One of Provenzano Salvani's friends being taken prisoner by Charles of Anjou, and 1000 golden florins being demanded in museum, Provenzano, subduing his natural haughtiness, stood in the Piazza of Sienna, and begged aid from the passers-by to raise this sum.

CANTO XII.

V. 25.—"*And here I saw who noblest aspect wore.*"
Lucifer, Son of the Morning.

V. 28 —"*And there I saw the great Briareus die.*"
The hundred-handed giant. (*See* Inferno, Canto XXXI. v. 98.)

V. 43 —"*O mad Arachne, there I saw thee still.*"
Arachne excelled so much in making tapestry, that she challenged Minerva to a trial of skill, and being defeated, was changed into a spider. From her name both the French *araignée* and the Italian *ragno* are derived.

V. 50, 51.—"*How well Alcmæon paid, in vengeance dire,
The gems his mother won for evil fate.*"
Alcmæon was son of the soothsayer Amphiaraus (see Inferno, Canto XX. v. 34) and Eriphyle. Amphiaraus knowing, by his powers of divination, that he must die before Thebes, hid himself; but Eriphyle, bribed by Polynices with a necklace which had been formerly given to Harmione by Venus, betrayed her husband's place of concealment. Amphiaraus therefore charged Alcmæon to revenge his death; and in obedience to his father, he murdered his mother.

V. 55-57.—"*The deed of cruel fierceness I behold,*
    Done when Tamyris unto Cyrus said ·
    For blood thou thirstedst, now with blood be
    fill'd."

Tamyris, or Thomyris, Queen of the Massagetæ. After her husband's death she marched against Cyrus, vanquished his army with great slaughter, and killed him on the spot. She then caused his head to be cut off, and thrown into a vessel full of human blood, saying, "*Satia te sanguine quem sitisti.*"

V. 80, 81.   ———"*again the footsteps turn*
    Of the sixth maiden on the hand of Day."

That is, it was the sixth hour, or about noon, counting the hours of day from sunrise. In all ages poets and painters have represented the God of Day preceded by Aurora, and attended by the blooming band of Hours.

V. 102-104.—"*As, when ye try the arduous heights that bring*
    Your steps unto the church that looks adown,
    Where Rubaconte o'er the flood doth fling
    His arch, amid the nobly guided town."

The Ponte di Rubaconte (now Ponte alle Grazie), on the Arno, at Florence, received its earliest name because built under the direction of Messer Rubaconte di Mandella, a Milanese, when he was Podestà or Magistrate of the city, in 1237. It is the most easterly of all the bridges, and, of course, the farthest up the stream; immediately behind it rises the steep hill on which the church of San Miniato is built, commanding a lovely view of Florence and the Val d'Arno. Dante calls Florence "nobly guided," in bitter irony.

V. 106 — "*When fraud in secret or cask was yet unknown.*"

An allusion to frauds committed in Dante's time. One Messer Niccola Acciaiuoli, in 1299, in league with Messer Baldo d'Aguglione, falsified the public books, tearing away a leaf which would have proved their dishonesty. Also Messer Durante de' Chiaramontesi, who held office in the custom-house, falsified the standard measure, substituting a cask of different size, and appropriating the profits to his own use

----

CANTO XIII.

V. 3 — "*Where for the second time recedes that hill*"

Dante had now attained the second zone, where the envious are punished As he supposes the mountain of Purgatory to be of a conical form, the circles, as they ascend, recede like terraces, one above another.

V. 9. — "*The stone was of a dull and livid hue*"

To show the joylessness of envy.

V. 29. — "' *Vinum non habent,*' *said.*"

Biagioli observes that Dante here distinguishes three degrees of charity First, to help those who need it; and of this he gives the example of Mary, who, at the marriage in Cana of Galilee, said "They have no wine." Secondly, to put oneself in peril, even of death, for the sake of others, of which the devotion of Pylades to Orestes is here given as an example. Thirdly, to return good for evil.

V. 33 — "A voice 'I am Orestes' cried"

These are the words of Pylades, who, when Orestes was condemned to death by the tyrant Ægisthus, cried, "I am Orestes," in order to save his friend.

V. 70, 71. — "For, 'neath their brows, an iron thread did sew / The lids together"

As the envious, in life, could not endure to look on the happiness of others, so here they may not look on the light of day.

V. 97. — "Among the rest, I saw a Shade," &c.

This Shade was a lady of Sienna, but authorities are divided as to her family name. Some say that she was wife of Cino de Figezza. Pietro di Dante calls her Sapia de' Provenzani, and Boccaccio, Sapia de' Salvani. She may possibly have been related to Provenzano Salvani (see Canto 11 v 111), and her joy at his defeat and death does not at all prove anything against this supposition ; for in those days, relationship by no means implied peace and harmony. It seems certain, however, that she was banished from Sienna, to Colle, a small town near Volterra ; but the cause of her exile is not known. Be that as it may, she bore in consequence such bitter hatred towards her fellow-citizens, that she rejoiced greatly at the defeat they met with in June, 1269, near the town to which she had been exiled.

V. 124-126. "*If, in his prayers before the throne of grace,*
Pietro Pettignano had forgot
His pity for my sad and evil case."

Pietro Pettignano, a hermit of the order of St. Francis, and nearly contemporary with Dante.

V. 148-150.—"*Thou shalt behold my friends among the band*
Who trust on Talamone; hope more vain
Than d'on in seeking Dian's fount doth stand."

That is, her relations and friends were among those who rejoiced on account of having acquired the castle and port of Talamone, on the Tuscan coast, by means of which they expected to become powerful at sea; a hope more vain than that of those who spent large sums of money in searching for a well which the Siennese believed to exist below their city. It appears, however, that in after times this well was actually found; for in the church of St. Nicholas, in the highest part of the town, there is said to be a well of extraordinary depth, called the well of Diana

---

CANTO XIV.

V 7.—"*Two spirits, on each other bending low*"

One of these spirits is Guido del Duca, of Bertinoro; the other Rinieri de' Calboli, of Forlì.

V. 16, 17.—" *There is a Tuscan stream, whose source*
    That hath its mountain-source in Falterona."

The Arno, which rises in a mountain called Falterona, among the Apennines, near the borders of the Romagna.

V. 22.—" *The soul to whom he spake, this answer made* "

Guido del Duca answers Rinieri de' Calboli.

V. 31-33.—" *For, mid the Alpine heights which most excel*
    In the rich store of forests, and whence is risen
    Peloros," &c.

"The Alpine heights" here mean the Apennines; which but for the straits of Messina, would be joined to Cape Peloros (now Cape Faro) in Sicily.

V. 43.—" *In truth, of them as of foul swine I deem.*"

By the swine, Dante here means the inhabitants of the Casentino.

V. 46.—" *Next it descends 'mong wretched curs.*"

The citizens of Arezzo.

V. 50.—" *Finds that the dogs to savage wolves have grown.*"

The wolves are the Florentine Guelphs. The word *Guelph*, in old German, means a *wolf*.

V. 52.—" *And then by darker gulfs it rushes down.*"

Through the narrow gorge of the Gonfolina, between Florence and Pisa.

V. 52.—*"And feeds the forms, with sharp cunning fill'd."*

The Pisans, whom the Florentines always accused of cunning, and by whom, indeed, they had been more than once over-reached.

V. 58, 59.—*"One of thy lineage, at no distant day,*
      These wolves from the proud river's bank shall drive."

Fulcieri de Calboli, when Podesta, of Florence, in 1302, was induced, by the bribes of the Neri, to persecute the Bianchi.

V. 64.—*"Bloody, from the drear wood he issues forth."*

The wood, or wolves, is generally the symbol of Florence.

V. 97, 98.—*"Where are Manardi, Lano the Good,*
      And Traversara and Carpegna now?"

Arrigo Manardi, of Faenza, or, according to others, of Bertinoro, he was noted for prudence, liberality, and magnanimity. Lano the Good was Messer Lino de Valbona, a brave and virtuous knight. Pier Traversaro, a good and great noble of Ravenna, one of whose daughters married Stephen, king of Hungary. Ovido di Carpegna, a noble of Montefeltro, noted for his great liberality.

V. 100-102.—*"When shall Bologna a new Fabbro show?*
      And Bernardin di Fosco in Faenza,
      Where from small seed a noble stem did grow?"

This Fabbro was one Domenico Fabbro de Lambertazzi, of Bologna, a citizen of low birth, but great virtue and talent. Fabbro, in Italian, means smith, and some are of opinion that it does not stand here as a proper name, but that the individual in question really was a smith, called Lambertaccio, who, from low degree, had nearly risen to be lord of Bologna. Bernardin di Fosco, of Faenza, also a man of the people, but distinguished for his good and noble qualities.

V. 104 —"*To weep at Guido della Prata's name.*"

Guido of Prata, a place between Ravenna and Faenza, was noted for his liberality and valour.

V. 105 —"*And Ugolino d'Azzo, with us once.*"

Commentators are divided as to who Ugolino d'Azzo really was. Some say that he was of the illustrious family of the Ubaldini of Florence, others that he was of Faenza, and plebeian in origin.

V. 106 —"*Tignoso, and the band who with him came.*"

Federigo Tignoso, a virtuous noble of Rimini, who lived, for the most part, in Bertinoro. Some commentators suppose "the band who with him came" to be his family and relations; others, a band of friends, chosen by him on account of their virtues and congenial dispositions.

V. 107.— "*The Anastagi, Traversaro's race.*"

The Anastagi were of Ravenna, related to the Polenta family. Traversaro's race, a distinguished family, also of Ravenna (see note to v. 96)

V. 112.— "*O Bertinoro, wherefore didst not flee!*"

Now Bertinoro, a small town of the Romagna, between Cesena and Forli.

V. 116-118.—"*In sooth 'tis well that heirs there should be none
In Bagnacavallo ; and to bring forth seed,
Como and Castrocaro ill have done.*"

Bagnacavallo, a village and castle of the Romagna, not far
from Ravenna. In Dante's time it was governed by its own
Counts, who do not appear to have been particularly estimable.
It was anciently called Tiberiacum, in honour of Tiberius.
Como, now destroyed, was also a castle of the Romagna, and
governed in the same manner as Bagnacavallo. Castrocaro, a
small town in the Romagna, near the Tuscan frontier, governed
like those above mentioned. It is now celebrated for its
mineral waters, which contain sodine. Its ancient name was
Salsubium.

V. 119, 122.—"*Though, when their demon-father homes shall speed,
Pagani's sons may prosper.*"

Mainardi Pagani, lord of Imola and Faenza, was, on account
of his extreme wickedness, surnamed *Il Demonio*. His evil fame
always hung like a dark cloud over his sons, although they
governed comparatively well, and prospered to a certain extent.

V. 122.—"*O Ugolin de' Fantoli,*" &c.

Ugolin de' Fantoli, celebrated for his virtues and noble
character. He had no children, and therefore the Poet con-
gratulates him that his name could never be disgraced by the
crimes of his descendants.

V. 144.—"*I am Aglauros, who was turn'd to stone.*"

Aglauros, daughter of Cecrops ; she was jealous of Mercury's
love for her sister, and was therefore turned into a stone.

CANTO XV.

V. 1—5.—" *As much as, 'twixt the third hour of the day*
And dawn, appeareth of the heavenly sphere,
Which ever moveth as a child at play,
There seem'd, as now the eventide drew near,
The same, ere yet the sun should sink to rest."

That is, it was three hours before sunset.

V. 6.—" *The hour of vesper there, and midnight here.*"

That is, in Purgatory it was the hour of vespers, not what is commonly, in poetry, called the vesper hour, by which is usually meant the rising of the evening star, but the hour at which vespers are sung in the Roman Catholic churches, i.e., three in the afternoon. Dante thus supposes it to be midnight in Italy at three p.m. in Purgatory.

V. 43—45. ——— " *I would fain*
Know what the spirit of Romagna meant,
Speaking of place and consort?"

Guido del Duca (see Canto XIV. v. 85)

V. 53.—" *But lo! we had attain'd the higher sons.*"

Where the wrathful are purified.

V. 97, 98. ——— " *If thou be ruler of the bourne*
Whose name among the Gods stirr'd up much strife,"

Athens, concerning the name of which disputes arose between Neptune and Pallas.

V 100, 101.   *"Revenge thee, Pisistratus, on the left
                      Of him who dared our daughter to embrace."*

These are the words of the wife of Pisistratus, tyrant of
Athens. She demanded vengeance against a youth who had
kissed her daughter in public

CANTO XVI.

V 46 —*"I was a Lombard ; Marco was my name."*

Commentators are divided on this subject, and few adopt
what would at first sight seem the simplest reading, viz , that
this Marco was a native of Lombardy. Boccaccio says that he
was of the Lombardi family, of Venice, *"uomo di Corte e
savio,"* which may be translated, a skilful diplomatist. Some
say that he was called the Lombard, because of the high favour
he held with the lords of Lombardy ; others suppose that
Lombard is here used as synonymous with *Italian*. But all
agree in stating him to have been a man of great talents and
irritable to excess. Portirelli conjectures that he may have
been no other than the far-famed Marco Polo. Here, however,
two insuperable difficulties arise. Firstly, that celebrated tra-
veller is stated by his biographer, the Abbate Zurla, to have
been a man of a singularly sweet and gentle disposition ; there
fore Dante certainly would not have placed him among the
wrathful Secondly, Marco Polo was still alive in 1323, as
appears by the date of his will , therefore, in 1300 he could not
have been in Purgatory at all

V. 64, 65 —" *For one in heaven, another on the earth*
Would place it."

That is, one imputes the evils of this world to the influence of the stars, another to the natural wickedness of man.

V. 86. —" *The soul comes forth, mantvll'd, unknowing aught* "

Without intentional imitation, it is possible that this passage of Dante may have suggested to Wordsworth some of the thoughts in his magnificent Ode on Immortality, especially the lines beginning—

"*Our birth is but a sleep and a forgetting* "

V. 99, 100 ——— "*your chief the hoof doth not divide,*"
Though verily he ruminates at will "

In allusion to the command to the Jews to abstain from eating the flesh of any animal that did not both divide the hoof and chew the cud. The latter is here supposed to symbolize the contemplative virtues, the former the active duties of life. Dante thus accuses the Head of the Church of neglecting good works.

V. 117 —" *There where the Po and Adige do flow* "
That is, Lombardy, the Romagna, and the March of Treviso

V. 118. —" *Ere Frederick into strife and discord fell* "
Before the wars of the Emperor Frederick II

V. 124-127.—"*Gherard the Good; Conrad Palazzo, him
Best call'd, in French, true Lombard; but
whom ye,
Besides, do Guido da Castello name.*"

Guido da Castello, a poet of Reggio, in North Italy. He
was of the noble family of the Roberti, who, according to
Benvenuto da Imola, hospitably received and lodged Dante
during his exile. It seems the French were at that time in the
habit of calling all the Italians *Lombards*. Conrad da Palazzo
was a Brescian noble; Gherard was a native of Treviso, and
was surnamed, for his virtues, the Good.

V. 141, 142.—"*If from his daughter Gaia be not drawn
Some appellation.*"

Gaia, daughter of Gherardo, appears not to have inherited
her father's good qualities; thus, any appellation derived from
her must have been a disgraceful one.

CANTO XVII.

V. 20, 21.—"*She who, for guilt, was doom'd the form to wear
Of the sweet bird whose song doth most delight.*"

Philomela, daughter of Pandion, King of Athens, and sister
of Progne, who married Tereus, King of Thrace. Philomela, as
is well known, was transformed into a nightingale, and Progne
into a swallow.

V. 34.—"*Before me a fair maiden seem'd to weil*"

Lavinia, daughter of King Latinus. Her mother, Amata,
promised her in marriage to Turnus, King of the Rutuli. The
gods, however, opposed this union, and the oracles declared
that she must become the wife of a foreign prince. Latinus,
accordingly, offered her to Æneas, but Turnus, enraged at this,
flew to arms, and Latium was the seat of the war. After much
slaughter, it was agreed that the quarrel should be decided by
single combat; and Æneas, being the victor, married Lavinia,
while Amata, in despair at being separated from her daughter,
hanged herself.

V. 62-64.—"*Strive to ascend, ere comes the twilight dim
For else we may not, till the dawning light,
Return*"

None might continue the ascent after the sun had set; thus
showing that, without Divine Light, none can climb the path
of penitence. "The night cometh, when no man can work."

V. 98, 99.—"*First, love the best; then, be in measure worn
The second.*"

That is, love first the things of heaven; then, those of earth.

CANTO XVIII.

V. 49.—"*Each form substantial*"

In the original, "Ogni forma sustanzial." This is an expression of the Schoolmen, and signifies that which, united to

sample matter, forms the different species of bodies. The
Atomists believed that there was a power or essence, or, in the
old phraseology, a virtue, which acted on the inert mass of
matter, and thereby produced the forms of everything that
exists in the world.

V. 73, 74.—" And noble virtue Beatrice doth name
Volition."

In the fifth Canto of the Paradiso, where she speaks of free
will as the greatest gift of God.

V. 79-81.—" And, 'gainst the sky, did by that pathway go,
Lit by the sun, when those of Rome behold
'Twixt Sards and Corsenans it lying low."

Against the apparent course of the sky the moon passed along
the Zodiac, through the sign of Scorpio, in which the sun is
when it appears to the Romans to set in the direction of Corsica
and Sardinia.

V. 82, 83.—" And he by whom Pietola doth hold
A nobler name than e'er the Mantuan town."

Virgil was born at La Pietola, a little village, generally
called Andes, it is about two miles from Mantua. One of the
Gonzagas built a palace there, to which he gave the name of
Virgiliana.

whom the multitude rushed wildly along, bearing torches, and
shrieking *Io Bacche.*

V. 100 — "*With haste did Mary to the mountains fly.*"

"And Mary arose in those days, and went into the hill-
country with haste."—*Luke* i. v. 39.

V. 112.—"*I was the Abbot of St. Zeno once,*" &c.

Commentators are divided as to the name of this Abbot of
St. Zeno: all, however, are agreed that he was a good man, but
deficient in energy, *molto remisso,* Landini says.

The church of St. Zeno is one of the most interesting in
Verona.

V. 120, 121.—"*Who hath made Milan weep her sore mischance,
The excellent Barbarossa*"

Milan did indeed suffer terribly at the hands of Frederick
Barbarossa, here ironically called good. He razed it to the
ground; and on Palm Sunday, 1162, the site of the once great
city was to be recognised only by the Basilica of St. Ambrose,
some few other churches, and three or four old Roman columns,
left standing in the midst of the ruins; while, the inhabitants
being dispersed in four adjoining villages, the name of Milan
was effaced from the Lombard community.

V. 122-124 ——"*one
Who soon shall mourn that o'er his hand hath sway
Upon our assent,*" &c.

The Abbot of St. Zeno here speaks of Alberto della Scala,
lord of Verona, who died in 1301, and was, in 1300, already old

and infirm. In 1292 he had expelled the lawful abbot, and forcibly introduced his own son in his place. This son, Giuseppe by name, was deformed and illegitimate.

V. 134, 137.—"*And those who, weary of the toil they bore,*
Slothful, did from Anchises' son depart."

Those Trojans who, weary of the long voyage, remained in Sicily, instead of going on with Æneas to Latium.

CANTO XIX.

V. 1.—"*Now when the heat of day no more hath power.*"
It is always coldest just before dawn.

V. 4.—"*When magic saw its greatest fortune gleam.*"

Magicians sometimes read the future in this manner: blindfolded, they marked the earth with the point of a rod, and then observed which of the constellations these random strokes resembled. If they bore the form of the stars which compose the end of Aquarius and the beginning of Pisces, they called it "the sign of greatest fortune." At the time of Dante's journey through Purgatory the sun was in Aries; consequently, a little before dawn, Aquarius and part of Pisces must have been above the horizon.

V. 19.—"*She sung, 'I am the Syren of sweet sound.'*"

The isles where the Syrens sang to Ulysses are still pointed out, off the coast of Amalfi. They are small, barren rocks, but

the wondrous beauty of the scene around might well have
detained the weary mariner, even without the Syren song

V. 26. —" When One appear'd in holy light array'd "

Some have supposed this to be Holy Truth ; others, Lucia, or
Divine Light.

V 22 — " And show'd to me the loathsome form within."

Spenser has here borrowed from Dante.

V. 99.—" I was, on earth, the heir of Peter's sway "

Pope Adrian V., by birth Ottoboon de' Fieschi.

V. 100-102 —" Between Chiaveri's and Sestri's bosoms
  Flows a fair stream, and from its name is known
  The title by my ancient lineage worn."

The river Lavagna, which flows between Chiaveri and Sestri,
and from which the Fieschi family take their title of Counts of
Lavagna.

V 136, 137. —" If e'er the holy evangelic word,
  That ' Neque nubent' said, were understood."

The words neque nubent are taken from Matt. xxii v 30, and
are here used to signify that not only marriage, but all other
earthly relations are at an end in the world of spirits.

V. 143 — " I have a niece, Alagia."

Alagia Fieschi, of Genoa, wife of Moroello Malaspina, the
friend and patron of Dante

CANTO XX.

V. 10 —" *O ancient wolf, be thou for aye accurst,*"

The wolf is here, and in many other passages, the symbol of avarice.

V. 25–27 ———— " *Fabricius, thou*
Didst rather poverty with virtue seek,
Than riches whereunto foul crime did grow "

Fabricius, the celebrated Roman, who refused the bribes of Pyrrhus. Although immense wealth had been won in his victories over the Samnites and Lucanians, and the treasury, and even the private soldiers, were enriched thereby, he took nothing for his own share, and always remained poor. He never used plate at his table, and the only silver vessel which he possessed was a small salt-cellar, whose feet were of horn. He always preserved the greatest simplicity in his way of life, saying that he wished rather to command those who had money than to acquire it himself.

V. 31, 32.—" *Now he recounted the great largess shed*
By Nicholas, upon the maidens three."

St. Nicholas, Bishop of Myra, who presented a father with dowries for his three daughters, in order that they might marry honourably.

V 46, 47.—" *If there were power in Douay, Bruges, Lille,*
Or Ghent, full soon revenge ye should behold."

These Flemish cities were taken possession of by Philip le Bel, partly by force and partly by treachery, in 1300.

V. 49 —" When erst on earth, Hugh Capet was I call'd."

The speaker is Hugh the Great, father of Hugh Capet

V. 52.—" I of a Paris butcher was the son."

This is by no means literally true, for Hugh, Duke of France and Burgundy, Count of Paris, Anjou, and Orleans, was, in rank and birth, second only to the sovereign. His family had, however, the privilege of providing the city of Paris with bullocks, or, as it would now be called, the monopoly of beef. Hence this epithet applied by Dante.

V. 53, 54 —" For when the ancient kings had pass'd away,
        Save one, in dusky raiment, all alone."

It is uncertain what is here meant by " in dusky raiment, all alone," but it is probably used metaphorically to express the misfortune and imprisonment of Charles the Simple. By " the ancient kings," the Carlovingian dynasty is meant.

V. 60, 61.   ——" But when the dower
        Of fair Provence destroy'd all modest shame,"

The dower here alluded to was, first, the wealth and lands of the Count of Toulouse, which France acquired by the marriage of the heiress of Toulouse with Alphonso, brother of St. Louis, in 1236, and, secondly, those of Raymond Berenger, Count of Provence, left by him to his youngest daughter Beatrice, married in 1245 to Charles of Anjou, also brother of St. Louis. But the whole of Provence, properly speaking, was not finally annexed to the crown of France till more than two centuries later, in the reign of Louis the Eleventh.

V. 64, 66   —— "of arvad, to make amends,
    Ponthieu and Gascony and Normanland."

It is not easy to reconcile the chronology of some parts of this passage with the known history of France. For instance, Philip Angustus conquered Normandy twenty-four years before any Provençal lands were acquired; yet Dante here gives the impression of the former being seized subsequently. It may be observed, that Dante does not say that France retained all the possessions here mentioned; on the contrary, she made use of them to increase her power and influence in Europe, by bestowing them as dowries on the daughters of the royal house.

V. 67 69 — "*And sent, in Italy, to make amends.*
   Charles slew Conradin , to heavenly life,
   St. Thomas then he sent, to make amends."

Charles of Anjou put the young Conradin to death, in 1268. Conradin's mother, Margaret of Austria, who brought a ransom too late to save him, employed the money in building the church of Santa Maria del Carmine, in the Piazza del Mercato in Naples. In this church is an exquisite statue of Conradin, modelled by Thorwaldsen. As to the other crime here imputed to Charles, it was said that he caused St. Thomas Aquinas to be poisoned, for fear lest, at the Council of Lyons, he might give an opinion contrary to his royal wishes; but the truth of this accusation is by no means proved.

This whole passage is eminently Dantesque, with its triple repetition of the phrase "to make amends." In the original it stands thus —

  " *Li comandò con forza e con menaggia*
  La sua ragion , e poscia, per ammenda,

> Ponß e Normandia prese, e Guascogna.
>   Carlo venne in Italia, e per ammenda,
> Vittima fe di Curradino; e poi
>   Ripinse al ciel Tommaso, per ammenda."

V. 73.—"*I saw another Charles come forth from France.*"

Charles of Valois, known by the name of Charles Sans Terre, who, by invitation of Boniface VIII, came into Italy in 1301, and was sent to Florence, on the pretext of pacifying the city. In this undertaking he was wholly unsuccessful.

V. 77, 78.   ——"*and that so much more grievous,*
  As if to have a lighter aspect were."

That is, the evil which shall befall him will be all the more serious, since he thought it a light matter to do evil to others.

V. 79, 80.—"*The other, newly captured on the wave,*
  I now behold   he doth his daughter sell."

Charles II. of Sicily and Apulia, who was taken prisoner in a naval battle by Ruggieri Doria, Admiral of the Arragonese fleet. Charles had a daughter called Beatrice, whom he gave in marriage, for the sum of 80,000 florins, to the Marquis Azzo VIII of Este, already old and infirm.

V. 86.—"*Within Alagna comes the flour-de-lys.*"

Alagni, now Anagni, a town to the south of Rome, between Valmontone and Ferentino. It was anciently the capital of the Hernici, and is described by Cicero, in his defence of Milo, as a "mundicipium ornatissimum;" also by Virgil as a wealthy city. In the Middle Ages it was the favourite residence of several Popes and Antipopes, and was the scene of the conclave which, after receiving the furious letter of Frederick II. calling the cardinals sons of Belial, elected Innocent IV. It was the birthplace of Stephen VII., Innocent III., Alexander IV, and Boniface VIII (Benedetto Caetani). The latter, after his quarrel with the Colonnas, against whom he had launched the fiercest anathemas, was involved in that memorable strife with Philip le Bel, in which the French clergy obtained their peculiar privileges. Philip was not inclined to submit to the pretensions of the Church, and Guillaume de Nogaret (whom some commentators believe to be represented by Dante as Geryon, in the seventeenth canto of the Inferno) invaded the Papal States, and allied himself with the Colonnas. The gate of Anagni was opened to them by treachery, and the French entered the city, September 7, 1303, crying · "Vive le roi de France, et meure Boniface!" The Pope, however, sustained no personal injury, and after three days the people recovered from their first surprise, drove out the French, and set Boniface at liberty. He hastened to Rome, and put himself under the protection of the Orsini, the hereditary enemies of the Colonnas, but was soon afterwards found dead in his bed.

V. 92.—"The lawless hands upon the temple fall."

Alluding to Philip le Bel's cruel persecution of the Templars.

V. 97.—"Know, what I spake of her, the Blessed Spouse."

See v. 22-36.

V. 162 — " We sing the story of Pygmalion's pride "

Pygmalion, not the celebrated sculptor of that name, but a king of Tyre, son of Belos, and brother of Dido. At the death of his father he ascended the vacant throne, and soon became odious by his cruelty, pride, and avarice. He sacrificed everything to his ambition, and even killed Sichæus, Dido's husband, only because he was the most powerful and opulent of all the Phœnicians. This murder he committed in a temple of which Sichæus was the priest; but Pygmalion did not thereby obtain the riches which he desired, for Dido, to avoid further acts of cruelty, fled with her husband's treasure to the coast of Africa, where she founded Carthage. Pygmalion died in the fifty-sixth year of his age, and the forty-seventh of his reign.

V. 206. — " The wretchedness of Midas we unfold "

Midas, as is well known, asked of the gods that all he touched might become gold; his prayer was granted, and in consequence he would have died of starvation if the fatal gift had not been rescinded.

V. 113 — " We praise the scourge which Heliodorus chased."

It may be that this passage suggested to Raphael his wonderful fresco in one of the stanze of the Vatican.

V. 115. — " His name who Polydorus slew "

The name of Polymnestor, king of Thrace, who threw Polydorus, son of Priam, into the sea.

V 116, 117.　　　　　　——"*O Crassus, tell us now*
　　　　　　　(For well thou knowest it) how gold doth taste."

Marcus Licinius Crassus, famed for his riches and avarice.
He perished in his unfortunate expedition against the Parthians.
His head was cut off, and sent to Orodes, king of Parthia,
who poured molten gold into his mouth, saying "For gold
thou thirstedst, now drink thereof."

V. 130 —"*Last widely, sure, of old, was Delos driven.*"

Delos, one of the Cyclades. Latona here brought forth
Apollo or the Sun, and Diana or the Moon, therefore called
the eyes of heaven, and the island, which had till then
floated hither and thither on the waves, became immoveable.
The sanctity ascribed by the ancients to the altar of Apollo
at Delos is well known

————————

CANTO XXI.

V. 10. — "*Even thus, a Shade appeared to me.*"

The Shade of the poet Statius He was born about half a
century after Virgil's death, and was one of his warmest
admirers. In one of his poems he describes his visits to
Virgil's tomb, and mentions that he composed his verses
within its precincts. It would appear that he became a
Christian, but secretly, for fear of persecution.

V. 50 　　——"*nor Thaumas' daughter sweet.*"
Iris, or the Rainbow, daughter of Thaumas. She was the

emblem of Hope, and her office was to cut the last thread which unites the soul to the body. This most beautiful myth, like that other lovely tale of Psyche, shows that the old Greeks had a vision, though dim perhaps and distant, of the Immortality of the Soul.

V. 89 — "I, of Toulouse"

Dante erroneously supposes Statius to be a native of Toulouse ; he was born at Naples.

V. 91, 92 ——————"erst did I sing Of Thebes, then of Achilles, great in fight."

Statius is known by two epic poems, the Thebaid, in twelve books, and the Achilleid, in two, which latter remained unfinished at the time of his death.

CANTO XXII.

V. 42 — "In the sad tournament my fate were told."

In that place of Hell where the prodigal and the avaricious are punished, by rolling great weights against each other. It is described in the seventh canto of the Inferno.

V. 46, 47. — "Full many a soul at the last day shall rise With close-cut locks."

Alluding to the Italian proverb, which says of a spendthrift, that "he wastes all, even to his hair." (See Inferno, Canto VII. v. 57.)

V. 44, 55 —" *But when thou erst did sing the reeds affrays*
   Of them, Jocasta's double sons of woe."

The strife of the two sons of Jocasta, Eteocles and Polynices
(See note to Inferno, Canto XXVI. v. 54.)

V. 57.—" *There spake the Singer of the pastoral lays.*"

The author of the Bucolics.

V 58.—" *By that which Clio there with thee doth show.*"

In the beginning of the Thebais, Statius invokes the aid of
Clio, the Muse of History

V 70 —" *There where thou saidst 'The world its youth renews.'*"

This prophecy, taken from the Sibylline books, is applied by
Virgil to the birth of the son of Pollio, but some writers have
found there a foreshadowing of the Advent, then near at hand,
of the Redeemer

V 103.—" *The Greek the Muses loved in days of yore.*"

Homer

V. 107 —" *And Agatho.*"

A Greek tragic poet of the time of Euripides.

V. 109.—" *There dwells Simonides,*"

A celebrated poet of Cos, who flourished B C 538. He was
universally courted by the princes of Greece and Sicily, and,
according to one of the fables of Phædrus, he was such a
favourite of the Gods, that his life was miraculously preserved
when the roof of the house fell, during an entertainment, upon

all those who were feasting. He gained a poetical prize in the eightieth year of his age, and lived to be ninety. The people of Syracuse, who had hospitably received and honoured him while alive, erected a magnificent monument to his memory. It is said that he added four letters to the Greek alphabet. Some fragments of his poetry are still extant.

V. 111. —— " *Ismene with sad eyes* "

Ismene, a daughter of Œdipus and Jocasta. When her sister Antigone was condemned to be buried alive, by the tyrant Creon, Ismene insisted on sharing her fate.

V. 112. — " *Deipyle, Argia with no dwell* "

Deipyle, daughter of Adrastus, king of Argos. She married Tydeus (see Inferno, Canto XXXII. v. 130), by whom she had Diomed. — Argia, another daughter of Adrastus, married Polynices, brother of Eteocles, and, like Ismene and Antigone, was put to death by the tyrant Creon.

V. 115. — " *And she who show'd where Langia's fountain well* "

Hysiphyle, who showed the Argives the fountain of Langia to quench their thirst.

V. 118. — " *And med her sisters, Deidamia* "

The daughter of Lycomedes, king of Scyra, at whose court Achilles was concealed, in order to avoid joining the Trojan war.

V. 121, 122. — " *Four of the Maidens of the Day had fled,
And by his chariot-wheel the fifth did go* "

This passage may here suggested to Guido his exquisite representation of the Hours, in the Rospigliosi Palace, in Rome.

V 144 —" *The impulse which in Mary stirr'd.*"

At the marriage in Cana of Galilee, when she said : "They
have no wine."

CANTO XXIII.

V 25 —" *Less maugre Erisicthon's frame, I ween* "

Erisicthon, a Thessalian, who derided Ceres, and cut down
her grove. This impiety irritated the goddess, who afflicted
him with continual hunger. He spent all his possessions, in
order to obtain food, and at last devoured his own limbs. His
daughter had the power of transforming herself into whatever
animal she chose, and she made use of this artifice to maintain
her father, who sold her, after which, she assumed another
shape, and became again his property.

V. 39 —" *A Jewish mother on her infant fed.*"

This fact is mentioned by Josephus as taking place during
the siege of Jerusalem by Titus.

V. 82, 83 —" *And those who Omo on man's brow descry,
In there, in sooth, the M might well have known.*"

In the human face may be traced the letter M, with two O's
between the lines, thus forming the word Omo, or Man. The
two O's are the eyes ; the M is formed by the eyebrows and the
nose. The thinner the face, the more plainly may these letters
be seen.

V. 48.—" *Then did Forese to my gaze appear* "

Forese, brother of Corso Donati, and of Piccarda.

V. 87.—" *By my own Nella's love, with weeping fraught,* "

By the tears and prayers of his wife.

V. 96.—" *Of the Barbagia where she still doth dwell* "

Barbagia, a mountainous part of the island of Sardinia, where, it would appear, the inhabitants were noted for immorality. On this account, Forese compares it to Florence.

CANTO XXIV.

V. 10.—" *But where Piccarda is, now tell to me.* "

Piccarda, sister of Corso Donati. She became a nun of the order of St. Clare of Assisi, but her brother Corso, wishing to give her in marriage to one of the Tosa family, scaled the walls of the convent, carried her off, and obliged her to marry according to his wishes. Dante afterwards meets her in Paradise.

V. 19.—" *This Shade is Buonagiunta the Lucchese* "

A poet, or rimatore (literally, rhymer), of the family of Orbesani, or Urbicciani, of Lucca.

V. 21, 22.—" *And he whose meagreness doth most displease,*
Once Holy Church embraced. "

Martin IV., a native of Tours. He was a great epicure, and his favourite dish was composed of the eels of the lake of

Bolsena, stewed, with different spices, in the much-esteemed white wine called *Vernaccia*. He was Pope from 1281 to 1284

V. 28 —"*There Ubaldin di Pila seem'd intent.*"

Ubaldino degli Ubaldini, of Pila, a castle in the Mugello, or upper part of the valley of the Sieve, north of Florence. He was brother of the celebrated Cardinal Ubaldini, mentioned in the Tenth Canto of the Inferno, simply as "the Cardinal."

V. 30, 31 —— "*Boniface, to whom on earth was lent
Of many souls the pastoral rule and care.*"

Bonifazio Fieschi, of Lavagna, was Archbishop of Ravenna at the end of the thirteenth century.

V. 32, 33.—"*And him I saw, who erst within Forli
Drank the good wine with lesser thirst than here.*"

Marchese de' Rigoghosi, of Forli, who was much addicted to drinking. One day his servant told him that everybody said he was always drinking. "Why not," replied he, "if I am always thirsty?" *Marchese* is not here a title, but a Christian name.

V. 33.—"'*Gentucca*' then he murmur'd."

Commentators have disputed much as to the meaning of this passage. The best authenticated opinion, however, is that Gentucca was a young, beautiful, and noble damsel of Lucca, whom Dante afterwards loved during his exile.

V. 43, 44.—"*A woman now is born who yet no veil
Doth wear,*" &c.

At that time unmarried women in Italy did not wear the veil, which was peculiar to matrons. The natural explanation of this

passage is that Buonagiunta goes on speaking of Gentucca.
Some commentators, however, wishing to close their eyes to the
well-attested fact of Dante's subsequent unfaithfulness, not only
to the memory of Beatrice, but to the more obvious claims of his
wife, Gemma Donati, have supposed this maiden to be Alagia,
niece of Pope Adrian V, and afterwards wife of Moroello
Malaspina. But Alagia was a Genoese, not a Lucchese. Others
have supposed the whole passage to be metaphorical, and to
refer to the Bianchi faction.

V. 51.—" *Fair ladies, who have hearts attuned to love* "

This is the first line of one of Dante's canzoni in praise of
Beatrice. It is preserved in the Vita Nuova, where he speaks
of it thus :—" Forasmuch as many persons had gathered from
my appearance the secret of my heart, certain ladies who had
met together, drawn by delight in each other's society, knew my
heart well, because they had all witnessed my manifold discom-
fitures. Happening to pass where these noble ladies were
assembled, one of them called to me to approach. She who so
called me was most gay and pleasant of discourse, so that when
I joined their circle, and saw that my most gentle lady was
not among them, I recovered my courage, and, saluting them,
inquired what might be their pleasure. There were many
ladies there, some of whom were laughing among themselves,
whilst others regarded me as if in expectation of what I should
say. Others there were engaged in conversation, of whom one,
turning her eyes upon me, and calling me by name, addressed
me thus :—' Unto what end lovest thou this lady, seeing her
mere presence overwhelms thee ? Tell me, for of a surety the
end and aim of such a love must be of the strangest.' And
when she had thus spoken, not only she, but all the others,

fixed their eyes upon me, awaiting my reply. Thereupon I answered 'The end and aim of my love hath until now been the salutation of this lady, of whom belike you speak ; and in that salutation I found the bliss which was the aim of all my desires. But since it pleaseth her to deny it to me, Love, my liege lord, in guerdon of my fealty, has placed all my happiness in something which can in no wise fail me.' Thereupon these ladies fell to conversing among themselves, and as upon occasion we see rain falling mingled with fair flakes of snow, so did their words seem to me intermingled with sighs. And when they had talked together for a time, the lady who had previously spoken, once more addressed me thus —'Tell us, we beseech thee, wherein rests this happiness of thine ?' And I made answer thus —' In the words which speak the praises of my lady ' And she replied —'Speakest thou the truth, then those words which thou hast spoken, as expressive of thy state, must have been put forth by thee with some other purpose.' Whereupon, reflecting on these words, a sense of shame came over me, and I took my leave ; and as I went, I said within myself —' Since there is happiness so great in those words which speak the praises of my lady, wherefore did I bethink me of speaking aught else ?' And I determined for the future to take the praise of that most gentle being as the theme of my discourse , and after meditating long thereon, meseemed I had chosen a theme so much too lofty for my powers that I had not the courage to begin ; and thus for some days I wavered between the desire to write and the fear to make a beginning. Then it chanced that, walking one day along a road, by the side of which ran a clear and sparkling stream, I was seized with a desire to sing of her, so strong that straightway I began to consider in what terms I should couch my strain , and I thought it would be unmeet to sing of her, save to ladies and in the second person ; and not to every lady either, but only to such as were pure and noble. Thus, as it were spontaneously, the following words mounted to my lips

' *Fair ladies, who have hearts attuned to love* ' "

In the original the words are :

" *Donne, ch' avete intelletto d' amore* "

Dante then goes on to state that he treasured this line in his memory, and, a few days after, wrote the whole canzone, of which these words are the beginning.

This appears to have occurred at a time when Beatrice, for some reason, had passed him without her usual courteous salutation.

V. 54.—" *Of saying him who in new rhyme hath sung* "

Poetry written in any of the modern languages was, in Dante's day, called *new rhymes*, to distinguish it from the old, classic, unrhymed Greek and Latin verse.

V. 56.—" *That erst Guittone and the notary kept* "

Guittone of Arezzo, one of the earliest Italian poets, but apparently not highly esteemed by Dante. The notary was Jacopo da Lentino, another rhymer, who lived towards the end of the thirteenth century.

V. 82, 83. ———— " *The man whose guilt hath been most sore,*
Dragg'd by his horse, I see upon the ground."

Corso Donati, chief of the Neri, and one of the most violent men of that stormy time. Dante here supposes that he was thrown from his horse, and killed by being dragged in the stirrup. But, in fact, he was killed by some Catalan soldiers, at St. Salvi, a mile from Florence, September 16, 1308.

CANTO XXV.

V. 2, 3 — "*For noon had shone, and the fierce solar ray*
Gave place to Taurus; Night the Scorpion pass'd."

At the time of the vision of Dante, the sun was in Aries; therefore the Poet, instead of saying that the sign of Aries had already passed the meridian, says that the sign next to Aries, namely, Taurus, had reached it. Night, in the opposite hemisphere from Purgatory, was in Libra, and that sign had, in like manner, passed the meridian, and given place to Scorpio

V. 22, 23 — "*If Meleager thou of old hadst seen,*
Consuming with the burning of a brand"

Meleager, a celebrated hero of antiquity, son of Œneus, king of Ætolia, by his wife Althæa, daughter of Thestius. The Parcæ were present at his birth, and predicted his future greatness. Clotho foretold his courage, Lachesis his strength, and Atropos declared that he should live as long as the brand, then on the fire, was unconsumed. Althæa instantly snatched the log from the fire, and kept it carefully. Meleager, accordingly, grew in stature and in strength, and his fame spread over the whole land. He went with Jason to Colchis, in search of the Golden Fleece, and there and elsewhere won glory. At last, in some disputes arising from the famous hunt of the Calydonian bone, Meleager had the misfortune to kill two of his mother's brothers. This enraged Althæa, who, in a moment of anger, threw the brand into the fire, and as it burned away, the life of Meleager was consumed with it, and he died. This legend bears a curious resemblance to the superstitious accusation brought against witches in the Middle Ages; when it was believed, that they made wax images, and melted them at the fire; thereby melting away the life of their victims

---

CANTO XXVI.

V. 92.—"*I Guido Guerrazzi was*"

An early Bolognese poet. Dante highly esteemed him, and here calls him his father in the art of poetry.

V. 94, 95.—"*As, said the story of Lycurgus' wrath,*
The sons toward their mournful mother sprang"

Hypsipyle, when she fled from Lemnos, was seized by pirates and sold to Lycurgus, king of Nemæa. She was entrusted with the care of the infant son of Lycurgus, and, when the Argives marched against Thebes, they met Hypsipyle, and obliged her to show them the fountain of Langia (see Canto XXII. v 116). To do this more expeditiously, she laid down the child on the grass, and, in her absence, he was killed by a serpent. Lycurgus, enraged, was about to put Hypsipyle to death, when he was prevented by the arrival of her two sons, who saved her

V. 120.—"*The Limosin before him did advance.*"

Gerault de Bernell, of Limoges, a famous Provençal poet, who seems to have been more popular than Arnault Danïello whom Guido Guinicelli here praises.

V. 140 —"*So sweet to me thy courteous questioning.*"

The speaker is Arnaut, or Arnaldo Daniello, one of the most celebrated of the troubadours, and praised by Petrarch as well as by Dante. This whole passage, from the verse here quoted to the end of the canto, except the last line, is in Provençal, of which language Dante seems to have been a perfect master.

————————

CANTO XXVII

V. 1–5.—   "*As when the earliest radiance of the sun
            Dawns where its Maker shed his sacred blood,
            And 'neath the midnight Ebro forth adown,
            And noonday burns above the Ganges' flood,
            Thus was it now,*" &c.

According to Dante's system, at sunset in Purgatory, it was sunrise at Jerusalem, noon on the Ganges, and midnight in Spain.

V. 5 —"*Beati mundo corde*"

"Blessed are the pure in heart"

V. 39.—"*What time the mulberry was stain'd with red*"

According to the legend, the fruit of the mulberry was originally always white, until stained by the blood of Pyramus and Thisbe.

V. 104.—"*Know, I am Leah.*"

The symbol of the active Christian life, under the Old Testament dispensation, as Rachel of the contemplative life.

CANTO XXVIII.

V. 7.—"*A pleasant air, that seemed no change to know*"

This whole description is taken from St. Basil's Discourse on Paradise.

V. 20.—"*In the pine forest near to Chiassi's shore.*"

Chiassi, anciently Classis, about two miles from Ravenna, on the road to Rimini. The pine forest extends along the shores of the Adriatic for a distance of twenty-five miles. One part is still called the *Pineta de' Pasti*, from a tradition that it was Dante's favourite walk. These Italian pine forests are indeed delicious, with their soft, dry, sandy paths, sweet odours, and endless variety of light and shade.

V. 40.—"*A lady, singing all alone.*"

Matilda, the symbol of active Christian life under the New Testament dispensation.

V. 49-51.—" Thou dost unto my thought the memory bring
                 Of Proserpine, when her sad mother lost
                 Her smile, and she the gladness of the spring."

This passage of Dante may have suggested to Milton his celebrated description of Proserpine gathering flowers in the field of Enna. In the original it stands thus —

" Tu mi fai rimembrar dove e qual era
Proserpina nel tempo che perdette
La madre lei, ed ella primavera."

CANTO XXIX.

V. 40.—" Let Urania's starry train."

The Muse of Astronomy.

V. 78.—" Seven divers bands within the splendour were."

The seven gifts of the Holy Spirit

V. 81.—" In breadth, I think ten paces ye might go."

The " ten paces " are supposed to signify the Ten Commandments.

V. 84.—" Each with a lily diadem was crown'd."

The lily, ever the emblem of purity.

V. 92, 93.—" *Four living creatures in their traces came,*
  Their brows enwreath'd with freshest leaves, I
  ween."

The four Evangelists, the green wreaths signifying the freshness and living energy of their inspired words.

V. 101.—" *Ezra in Ezekiel,*" &c.

The living creatures described by Ezekiel had four wings, those seen by St. John in Patmos had six.

V. 107, 108 —" *A chariot borne upon triumphal wheels,*
  And harness'd to a flying griffin, came"

Dante uses the chariot as the emblem of the Church, the two wheels are the Old and New Testaments: the flying griffin, half lion, half eagle, is here the symbol of Jesus Christ, in whom are united two natures; the lion signifying the human, the eagle the divine.

V. 121 —" *At the right wheel three damsels seem'd to fly.*"

Faith, Hope, and Charity. Faith in snowy white, Hope with robes of emerald hue, and Charity all rosy red.

V 127, 128.—" *And now the white-robed maiden led the dance,*
  Now she of rosy hue"

Sometimes Faith takes the lead, and sometimes Love; but never Hope, which must follow, not precede, the others

V 130-132.—" *And, by the left wheel, then four pass'd along,*
  In purple robes; and she their steps who led
  Look'd from three visual orbs."

The four cardinal virtues, Prudence, Justice, Fortitude, and

Temperance; Prudence, having three eyes, to denote her great circumspection, guides all other virtues in their path.

V. 132.—"*I saw two ancient men,*" &c.

St. Luke and St. Paul; the former as the writer of the Acts of the Apostles, the latter of the Epistles.

V. 136, 137.—"*One seem'd to be a follower of him,*
The great Hippocrates."

Dante has already seen Hippocrates in Hades; and now calls that old Greek master of the healing art the instructor of Luke the beloved physician.

V. 139, 140.—"*With contrary intent, a burnish'd glaive*
Of sharp and glittering light the other held."

St. Paul is always represented with a sword, the sword of the Spirit.

V. 142.—"*Then four, in humble garments, I beheld.*"

Some commentators suppose these four to be St. Gregory the Great, St. Jerome, St. Ambrose, and St. Augustine; others, the Apostles James, Peter, John, and Jude. If the latter explanation be correct, this whole description must be taken as a personification of the books of the New Testament, rather than of their writers. The next verse renders this interpretation probable.

V. 143.—"*And following them, came an old man alone.*"

St. John, as writer of the Apocalypse.

CANTO XXX.

V. 1.—" *When the seven stars of Paradise on high.* **"**

The seven Lamps of the Spirit. Dante here compares them to the stars of Ursa Major, which point up to the pole, and therefore may always guide the mariner.

V. 123 —" *And ' Give such wealth of lilies,' did resound.* **"**

Literally, *handfuls of lilies.* Dante here quotes a line of the Æneid —

"*Manibus o date lilia plenis*"

V. 31-33 —" *With mass-attire veil and olive shadows,*
A Lady I beheld, 'neath mantle green,
Cloth'd in the colour of the living flame. **"**

Beatrice, who, the first time Dante saw her, wore, as he himself tells us, an apparel of a "most noble" crimson colour. The glowing crimson robe also signifies love, the white veil purity, the green mantle eternity, and the olive garland wisdom.

V. 34, 35 —" *And then my spirit, which so long had been*
Without the trembling thrill her presence bore. **"**

Ten years had elapsed from the death of Beatrice to Dante's supposed journey among the dead.

V. 49.—" *But Virgil was no longer by my side.* **"**

Human reason disappears in the presence of Divine Knowledge.

V. 55 — " *Dante, that Virgil from thy side hath gone.*"

This is the only occasion on which Dante ever mentions his own name in the whole course of the poem.

V 68.—" *By the olive leaves of Pallas.*"

The olive was sacred to Pallas

V. 83, 84.—" *And sang   'Speravi, Domini, in te ,'
           And stopp'd, nor beyond 'pedes meos' pass'd.*"

The 31st Psalm begins, in the Latin version, thus · "*In te,
Domine, speravi,*" in our Prayer-Book version, "In thee, O
Lord, have I put my trust." In the ninth verse the words
pedes meos occur   In the tenth verse the Psalmist passes from
praise to lamentation, which latter would have been unsuited
to the terrestrial Paradise.

V 85, 86.—" *As, on the living rafters which there is
           In Apennine*"

This expression exactly describes the roof-like form of the
crests of Italian pines.

V. 87.—" *Are heap'd by winds from the Sclavonian sea* "

That is, from the north-east

V. 89, 90.—" *When breathed on by the land whereon there has
           No shadow*"

By the sirocco, the wind of the African desert.

CANTO XXXI.

V. 73 —" *Or those which from Iarbas' kingdom blew.*"

Iarbas, King of Gætulia, from whom Dido bought land on which to build Carthage. Thus, the storms from Iarbas' kingdom are the wild tempests from the south-west, which blow with fearful violence on the coast of Italy.

CANTO XXXII.

V. 32, 33 —" *And then they circled round a tree, whose pride*
Of verdant leaves and blossoms all had fled."

This tree is supposed to mean the Roman Empire, in its corrupt state of heathenism; and its sudden blossoming, when the chariot is tied to the withered stem, represents the fresh life infused into the decaying empire after the introduction of Christianity.

V. 65, 66.—" *Here, at the tale of Syrinx, slumber fell*
Upon those eyes whose watching mark'd their woe."

Syrinx, a nymph of Arcadia, who was changed into a reed. Mercury sang this legend so sweetly to Argus, that he lulled him to sleep, and killed him. Juno then took his hundred eyes and put them on the tail of the peacock.

V. 99.—" *Which rufe from Aquilo and Auster 'fide.*"

Aquilo, the north wind; Auster, the south.

V. 112, 113.—" *As here I now behold the bird of Jove
Swoop on the tree.*"

The eagle is here an emblem of the Roman emperors who
persecuted the Christians.

V 118, 119 —" *And then, in the triumphal car there stood
A fox.*"

The fox is supposed here to signify the heretics of the first
ages of the Church, and is thus put to flight by Divine Knowledge, personified by Beatrice.

V. 124-126.—" *And then return'd once more within my sight
The eagle, and full swiftly cleft the bar,
And fill'd the chariot with its plumage bright.*"

Here Dante seems to allude to the Church's acquisition of
temporal power and wealth.

V. 130, 131.—" *And now it seem'd as from the earth there brake
A dragon,*" &c.

The dragon is generally supposed to be Satan, bearing away
the humility of the Church

V. 142-144   ———" *The holy edifice,
Transform'd thus, now divers heads put forth;
One at each side, three at the foremost place.*"

The divers heads are usually explained as being the different
vices incident to a state of earthly prosperity But this
passage is extremely obscure; indeed, the whole Canto is

difficult, and the explanations given should rather be called
conjecture. From v. 118 to the end, Dante apparently alludes
to the dealings of Bonifam VIII. with Philip le Bel, but the
metaphors are singularly inappropriate, beyond the waters of
Lethe, in the pure and sinless terrestrial Paradise.

CANTO XXXIII.

V. 1.—"_Deus, venerunt gentes._"

These words are the beginning of Psalm lxxix.

"_O God, the heathen are come into thine inheritance._"

**V. 36, 37.— "_That God's revenge doth tarry not, for sake
Of funeral sop_"**

Alluding to an ancient superstition, which taught that, if the
slayer could eat a sop at the grave of the slain within nine days
after the murder, he need not fear the vengeance of the relations. Here then Dante says, that though man may escape
punishment from his fellows, he cannot, by any device, escape
the vengeance of God.

V. 43 — "_When one who is five hundred, ten, and five_"

This passage has greatly exercised the ingenuity of commentators. Some have written the above-mentioned numerals in
Arabic characters, some in Roman, endeavouring to support
their different theories thereby. The most general opinion is
that the letters D U X are intended, forming the word _Dux_,
or _Leader_.

V 46, 47.   ——"*My salvation due*
                As Themis, or the Sphynx."

Themis, daughter of Heaven and Earth. Her oracle was famous in Attica, in the age of Deucalion.

V 49 —"*But soon events shall be the Naiades.*"

It would appear that we ought here to read *Laiades* for *Naiades*, and that the passage refers to the enigma proposed by the Sphinx to Œdipus, the son of Laius. The riddle was this —What animal walks on four feet in the morning, on two at noon, and on three at night? Œdipus replied that man goes on all fours in childhood, on two legs in the prime of life, and with the help of a staff in old age. Œdipus accordingly received the prize, viz. the crown of Thebes; but having previously killed Laius, in ignorance that he was his father, the country was, on his account, visited by famine, murrain, and pestilence. Thus Beatrice here says that events will explain her predictions without the misfortunes which attended the reign of Œdipus.

V 67, 68 —"*But thy vain thoughts, like Elsa's streams which flow*
                In petrifying waves "

Elsa, a small river of Tuscany, which flows near San Gemignano, and finally falls into the Arno. It possesses the property of petrifying whatever is steeped in its waters.

V 91, 92   ——"*No memory is mine*
                That I did e'er depart from love of thee."

Dante, having bathed in Lethe, has forgotten all sin and evil.

V. 92, 93 — "*Thus, thou in thy forgetfulness mayst seek,*
    And find the proof of all thy guilt and woe"

If there had been an evil in Dante's unfaithfulness to
Beatrice, he would not have forgotten it.

V 118 — "*Me seem'd, both Tigris and Euphrates burst.*"

Glanville (usually called Bartolomaeus Anglicus) cites an
assertion as made by St. Basil and St. Ambrose, that the water
of the fountain which proceeds from the Garden of Eden falls
into a great lake, and that from this lake proceed the four chief
rivers mentioned in Genesis   This passage is not to be found
in the known works of either of the above named authors, but
it seems to have been currently received as theirs during the
Middle Ages.   Washington Irving mentions that Columbus
derived thence his idea that the vast body of fresh water which
filled the Gulf of La Ballena, or Paria, flowed from the fountain
of Paradise, though from a remote distance , and that in this
gulf, which he supposed in the extreme part of Asia, originated
the Nile, the Tigris, the Euphrates, and the Ganges; which
might be conducted under the land or sea, by subterraneous
channels, to the places where they spring forth on the earth,
and assume their proper names

www.ingramcontent.com/pod-product-compliance
Lightning Source LLC
Chambersburg PA
CBHW020944030726
47496CB00005B/1345